POISONVILLE

In Padana City, with the death of the political parties and the Catholic parishes, power is no longer in the hands of members of parliament, prefects, mayors, bank presidents and association chairmen, CEOs, judges, and colonels. Power is in the hands of a few major families. It is an assembly made up of a few private business groups led by powerful citizens working together that constitutes the structural framework of power . . .

—GIULIANO RAMAZZINA,
Fuori Mercato, 2002

I t had been a Wednesday like any other. A winter Wednesday in northeastern Italy. During the day, the roads filled up with commuters and semitrailers. Long lines of vehicles crept along overburdened superhighways, national highways, and provincial roads. In Padua and Vicenza, as on so many Wednesdays before this one, air pollution was well above the legal limit. Long after sunset, the Mestre viaduct was still a grinding procession of heavy vehicles advancing slowly in both directions: a long smoky conveyor belt bringing freight—legal and illegal—from and to the countries that lie to the east. On that particular Wednesday, four more companies had gone out of business; the largest of the four employed fifty-one people. There were four more now-empty industrial sheds with "For Rent" signs, posted in Italian and in Chinese. Industrial sheds had been the subject of a lecture that morning: a professor of urban studies at the Department of Architecture, University of Venice, had told his class that, with the construction of 2,500 industrial sheds annually, the countryside had lost no fewer than 1,350 square miles of farmland, and that in the province of Treviso alone, there were 279 industrial parks, an average of four industrial sites per municipality. The professor was profoundly concerned; he told his students that the devastation being visited on the countryside was widespread and deep-rooted—and possibly irreparable. In the Northeast, the proliferation of industrial parks had wiped away the memory of the soil—the land—and people's identity. In another university classroom, the topic of discussion that Wednesday had been local identity. Three residents out of four continued to use the local dialect, even in professional settings. It was a reassuring statistic, according to the professor: local dialect was a significant factor in the preservation of community. And indeed, many colorful expressions in dialect were uttered during a conference held at the Museo dello Scarpone in Montebelluna, a foundation for the documentation of the local hiking-shoe and ski-boot industry. During the conference, it had been announced that forty-four local shoe manufacturing companies would begin outsourcing production. It's all China's fault, more than one attendee had said. Imports of leather footwear from China had risen seven hundred percent in the last year alone. The minister of industry had issued a call for the introduction of anti-dumping tariffs to discourage the phenomenon. Also, the Coldiretti, the association of Italian farmers, had issued a press release that Wednesday afternoon, expressing its concern over the skyrocketing rise in the importation from China of dried beans and and pickled vegetables, both of which had long been major sectors of production in several areas of the Northeast. That Wednesday, Chinese investors had also purchased a couple of storefronts and various local businesses. The Chinese always paid cash, and never haggled over the price. There had been considerable discussion of money, on the other hand, in various meetings where banking executives expressed their satisfaction with the positive trend in quarterly profits. Profits were also the topic of discussion at a press conference held by the tax police—specifically the profits of 262 tax evaders arrested in a recent sweep. In the course of that investigation, agents had also discovered 1,200 undocumented workers and 776 workers without valid residency permits. Many of those workers were immigrants without visas or work permits. Illegal immigrants, in fact, accounted for the majority of those arrested by the police across the Northeast.

For years, criminal cultures from Eastern Europe and the third world had established a local presence; in fact, Italian organized crime was only a fond memory of aging police-beat reporters. Prostitutes, defying the bone-chilling cold and the blanketing fog, had been out lining the provincial roads since the late-morning hours. In the evening darkness, they were everywhere, in villages, towns, and cities. Streetwalking was a flourishing business. Just like drug trafficking, for that matter. The sector that was suffering, on the other hand, was higher-end prostitution, in nightclubs and lap-dancing clubs. The nightclub owners had been the first to notice the symptoms of an impending recession. The manufacturers and professionals who once came out in droves, spending thousands of euros a night on champagne and escort services, were beginning to vanish from circulation. The only sector that was doing better than last year was wine production; wine exports had increased. That Wednesday, once again, hundreds of cases of Marzemino, Prosecco, Sauvignon, and other wines had been shipped to various places around the world. Politically speaking, the future was uncertain, though the recent elections had returned the incumbent regional administration to office. That day, there had also been meetings and secret sessions, both in the majority and among the opposition, in an attempt to reconcile internal conflicts and thwart reckless power grabs. It appeared that no one was capable of governing the future. It had been a Wednesday like any other. When midnight finally put an end to that Wednesday, a thick, milky fog reigned everywhere. The heart of the Northeast beat a little slower, taking refuge in the momentary respite of nighttime.

W hy isn't she here by now? It's almost one in the morning."

The wax sculpture that was taking shape in his hands couldn't give him an answer, even though the resemblance to her—with all the work he did on it—was becoming more unsettling day by day. The shaft of illumination from a small spotlight fell on that perfect, unearthly face. But something was still missing. And what was missing was a soul. How could he capture her soul? He wasn't really much good as a sculptor—to tell the truth, he wasn't much good at anything. And a sense of anxiety was devouring him; his artificial hip refused to tolerate all those hours on his feet. Even the scar on his cheek was pulsing, as if it were reawakening at night. Perhaps it was the thought of Giovanna, who in just nine days would be married to Francesco.

He reached a hand out to his work table and wrapped his fingers around one of the sharp metal tools that he had set to heat up in the flame of the spirit stove. He inserted the red-hot blade of the tool into the socket of the sculpture's right eye.

The eye, says the proverb, is the mirror of the soul, and he wanted to carve that soul out of her, if he ever succeeded in finding it.

"Why isn't she here by now?" he wondered once again, as the wax sizzled at the contact with the red-hot steel.

* * *

Despite the dense fog, she pressed her foot down hard on the acclerator, and the red Mazda hurtled along well above the legal limit. She knew that country road; she knew it very well. The last thing she was worried about was curves in the road. The man who had ruined her life, the man who had turned her into a slut, was waiting for her.

Just one more curve and she would be there, with him, for the last time. Her friend Carla was right. She couldn't marry Francesco without confessing the whole truth to him. But how could she tell him? What would happen? Would Francesco still want her?

Ugly thoughts kept proliferating in her brain like a metastasizing cancer, and she was losing control of the car. The idea that she might lose Francesco fell like a dark screen between her and the windshield. For a moment the road vanished. Her heart lurched into a whirlpool, just in time for her hand to make the imperceptible movement that took her back onto the straightaway, beyond the curve.

"Focus on driving, you stupid slut."

Her right foot, wrapped in an elegant piece of sexy, revealing footwear, lifted off the accelerator. The car lurched suddenly to a slower speed, and at the same time her heart lurched with it. If only she could save herself from her own thoughts with such exemplary speed.

But around that curve, at the end of the straightaway, he was waiting for her. The man who had ruined her life.

A glaring light in her rearview mirror blinded her thoughts. Once again, instinct made her wary, cautious. The headlights swerved to the left, the smoked-glass windows of a Jeep Cherokee were lowered, and savage howls poured out as the vehicle pulled up next to her. She knew she shouldn't turn her head to look but she couldn't help herself. It was only for an instant, long enough to glimpse a blurry figure gesticulating in the fog. Better not to accelerate, it would only give them an excuse to start a race, to get their pulses racing even faster. Soon she would be there.

Two hundred yards further along the road, Giovanna parked as close as she could to the elegant little villa. The Cherokee was parked on the far side of the roadway.

Just twenty quick strides and she would be at the front door.

Only five minutes earlier, it would have seemed inconceivable that she would be turning to him for safety. Her high heels slithered in all directions in the gravel. Walking in the gravel in those shoes was like climbing up a sand dune. The important thing was not to turn around. She heard nothing— no slamming car doors, no running footsteps behind her. It was not until she reached the front door that she decided to turn and look. The dark windows of the offroad vehicle had been rolled up, and at that point, she no longer even cared whether they were staring at her. Another instant and he would open the door and let her in. Fog and darkness. She leaned on the doorbell.

"Giovanna, at last you're here. I was so worried."

His reassuring voice.

She walked in and allowed herself to be embraced, resting her face against his chest, breathing in his aroma.

For a moment she no longer felt like his lover, his troublesome trollop, as he liked to call her. For a brief second, she felt like a daughter who had returned home after a nasty and frightening brush with danger.

It was in the aftermath, when he lifted her face with a finger under her chin and kissed her on the mouth, in the mouth, that his authoritative passion had once again made her swoon helplessly, lost, under his power.

Without a word, he had pushed her down onto the bed, and now he was thrusting inside her, the way she liked it. He was strong and confident. She didn't sense in him that anxious need to please her that she always felt from Francesco. He gave and he took, gave and took. That was the game they played. But then he took her soul and she had nothing left to give. Now she knew what she had to do. She had to push with all her might to lift that body off of her, free herself from its weight.

"No, that's enough! I don't want to do this anymore, that's enough! Did you hear me?"

He stopped. He looked into her eyes and understood.

He got up, freeing her of his weight, and sat on the side of the bed.

"It's over, isn't it?"

Giovanna didn't anwer. She delicately rested the tips of her fingers on his naked back.

He nodded wearily.

She hadn't expected it to be so easy.

But now here she was, lolling in a bathtub full of hot water, enveloped in a curtain of steam. Her mind drained of thoughts, her body protected in a warm liquid cradle. Ever since she was a little girl, she had loved hot baths. It seemed as if there were no safer place on earth.

The nicest moment of the day, when her mother kneeled in front of the tub to wash her hair. Her hair was blonder and longer then: it reached down to her hips. My little mermaid, her mother used to call her.

Childhood had been the only truly happy time in her life. Later, she had been forced to grow up in a hurry, without time to distinguish between men and boys, as if adolescence had been denied her. From teddy bears to a law degree had been a single dive from the Olympic platform—without even enough time to slip off her waterwings.

In town, people said that she had set her sights on

Francesco to make her way into the circles that mattered. Instead, what had really happened was that Francesco had given her back her adolescence. Even better, he had shown her what innocence was. Francesco had been her redemption. And that was why, the next day, she was going to tell him everything. Not to free herself of a burden, but for the sake of honesty. Out of love.

Once she had read a Japanese poem: "Take what is good. / Pile it in one dish of the scale. / Do the same thing with what is evil. / Balance the two dishes. / When the scale is level, you will know the exact weight of life."

If Francesco could find it in his heart to forgive her, their life together would be like those Sunday mornings when you wake up in the warmth of a comfortable bed, hear the rain outside, and have all the time you want to snuggle or fall asleep, smell nice smells, run your fingers over your smooth and well-rested skin, and feel happy. Happy that you've woken up.

The water was losing its warmth, but she hated to get out. She turned the faucet for more hot water. She closed her eyes, slipping into a pleasant slumber.

When she startled awake, she wasn't sure what had made her open her eyes. A gust of cold breeze, a shiver across her skin. The candle flame trembled.

He appeared in the doorframe, in shirtsleeves. For one happy moment she had forgotten about him. He had remained in the other room, sitting on the side of the bed. Without talking, without looking at her. She hoped he had gone away. Out of her life forever. She was so stupid. The Ativan tablet that she had swallowed before climbing into the bathtub, with a long sip of Armagnac as a chaser—that's why she felt so unconcerned.

The hot water kept pouring from the faucet; the tub was beginning to overflow.

He leaned over to turn off the water.

"Did you fall asleep?"

She watched as he sat on the edge of the tub, rolled up his sleeves, and squeezed some shampoo into his hand. She felt his hands slide delicately over her hair.

Like my momma—the thought emerged, absurd and incongruous.

His strong manicured hands ran through her hair, the hair that was much shorter than it had been when she was a girl all those years ago. His hands slid down her neck, to her shoulders.

"This is the last time you'll ever touch me. Tomorrow I'm telling Francesco everything."

The hands froze, motionless, resting on her shoulders.

"And so we put an end to this."

The hands rested for another moment. Then they shoved her under. The water tasted of jasmine, but it was salty. She would never have imagined he could be so strong. She managed to lift her head, but not enough to get her nose and mouth above the surface. Now he was in the tub; he had one knee braced against her sternum. She could feel the oxygen draining out of her chest, forming bubbles. Her eyes were burning. Her arms scrabbled along the walls of the tub. One leg surged out of the water. "Salt on my lips, the taste of the sea." The words of a song from the sixties surfaced in her mind, strangely. She felt a sharp pain, her heel slamming against the edge of the tub. Then nothing: her eyes opened on darkness. The last few little bubbles.

And the grieving moan of the man who had put an end to her life.

* * *

At night, the smaller train stations were deserted. Instead of ticket vendors and train dispatchers, everything was automated now: computerized machinery managed railroad traffic and issued tickets. That is why he had chosen the last train from Venice. No one was expecting him, no one could even have guessed he would arrive in town. He was certain they'd never see him. Even if he did happen to cross paths with someone, he could rely on the fog to provide concealment.

In that dense fogbank, he felt as if he were a damned soul in one of those circles of Dante's Inferno that he had studied, distractedly, in another lifetime. He pulled up the collar and lapels of his heavy jacket. As he felt his way through the darkness, navigating by instinct, he felt as if the enveloping mist were issuing from him. He thought back to the bull. The bull. He was ten years old, coming home from school. A bull had suddenly appeared before him, blocking his way. The bull must have been lost. It stood there, motionless, staring at him, snorting and puffing. He had never told another living soul about that meeting. For years, though, he had cherished the belief that the bull was a devil, and that the fog was an evil spell the demon employed to steal children away, without interference. Now, though, it was he who snorted and puffed in hatred. It was he who would use the fog to act, undisturbed.

He arrived in the main piazza, where he recognized the silhouette of the bell tower and the neon sign of the Bar Centrale. He dropped his heavy suitcase on the pavement. He turned slowly, looking all around him, and leaving to his memory the task of glimpsing each and every detail.

The noise of a car startled him. He grabbed his duffel bag and hurried into hiding in the portico. The vehicle, a Jeep Cherokee, began driving in circles around the piazza. From the lowered windows issued excited youthful shouts. Then, with a revving roar and a screech of rubber, the car accelerated away into the fog. He emerged from his hiding place and went in search of a phone booth. He found one next to the old newsstand. It was pitch dark; some little kid must have spent a half-hour amusing himself by shattering the fluorescent tubes. He pulled a lighter and a scrap of paper out of his pocket and, by the light of the little flame, read a phone number. The impersonal voice of an answering machine responded. The subscriber was not at home.

"Where the hell have you gone?" he shouted.

Only the fear of discovery obliged him to regain a measure of calm and caution. He slithered away under the porticoes like a sly old rat with a well-honed instinct for survival.

* * *

I'd been lying awake for a while, but I felt too queasy to try to get out of bed. I'd had too much to drink the night before. Gin-and-tonics and champagne. I could still smell the hostess's spicy perfume on my neck and chin. It wasn't going to be an easy morning. Luckily, I didn't have any court appearances scheduled; just a couple of office appointments. I looked over at the digital alarm clock for the tenth or eleventh time. I still had a few minutes left to try to get the alcohol out of my system. Then I'd bolt down an espresso, run a scalding hot shower, and be ready for another day on the job as a young lawyer. My friends had decided to throw me a stray party in the town's one and only nightclub. Giovanna would ask me how it had gone. In reality, she wanted to know whether I'd wound up in bed with one of the young women at the Club Diana. No, I hadn't. The party had been a flop. At least for me. Davide and the others had probably enjoyed themselves enormously. They were all pretty euphoric. They kept ducking in and out of the utility closet where one of the Romanians who worked at the club had lines of coke constantly at the ready. They had made perfect asses of themselves with the hostesses. The prettiest hostess, a Latin-American girl who—I think—was named Alicia, had been shoved into my arms, bedecked with ribbons and bows as though she'd been giftwrapped.

"She's not as pretty as Giovanna," Davide had told me. "But apparently she fucks divinely."

She'd done her best, but I was careful to keep things within limits. I'm a Visentin after all, and as my father had once reminded me, there are certain things we don't do.

"Not here in town, anyway," he'd added with a smile.

Moreover, there were a number of people I recognized, most of them small-time industrialists, their pockets stuffed with money. Some of them were clients of my father. Constantin Deaconescu, the owner of the club, a Romanian with a criminal air, had come over to give his best wishes for my wedding.

So all eyes were on me. I felt ill at ease, I didn't like the club one bit. It was as vulgar and pretentious as the brand of champagne that the waiters kept serving, in a sort of bucket brigade. When Alicia let her hands wander a little too far below the belt for my social position, whispering that she was entirely at my service—all night long—I looked at her carefully. She was beautiful and seductive, but at that moment I wished I were with Giovanna instead. I made an excuse, said that I must have had a little too much to drink, and stepped outside for a breath of fresh air. Behind me I heard a chorus of catcalls from my friends. It must have been two in the morning, and the icy chill in the air made me gasp. And there, stepping out of a sports car, was the last person on earth I wanted to see: Filippo Calchi Renier.

"What do you want?"

He pointed to the BMW. "Let's take a drive. I have to talk to you."

"Do you need a lawyer?"

He shook his head in annoyance. The scar on his cheek was bluish from the cold. "We need to talk about Giovanna."

"Of course," I muttered, as I turned and walked toward the sports car.

Filippo and Giovanna had been a couple a few years back.

Then she left him when she and I started dating. She broke the news to him one summer evening, at the festival in honor of the town's patron saint. He got in his car and drove off; a couple of hours later he plowed straight into an old oak tree that stood by the highway. He'd been driving at a recklessly high speed; he had a blowout and lost control of the vehicle. Or at least that was his version, but everyone in town speculated that he might have been trying to kill himself. He was never the same after that, physically or mentally. I just felt sorry for him. But for Giovanna, there was a sense of guilt that she just couldn't shake. She and I couldn't talk about him without starting a furious argument. Filippo was the only child of the Contessa Selvaggia Calchi Renier. His was the most prominent family in town; mine was the second-most prominent. I, too, was an only child. My mother had died about fifteen years ago. A tumor killed her. She died in a private clinic in California. All my father's money couldn't save her.

Filippo started the motor.

"We don't have to go anywhere," I said. "We can talk right here."

Filippo ignored me and put the car in gear.

"You can't marry her."

"The wedding's in nine days. You'd better get used to it."

"She doesn't love you."

"Let me guess: she loves you?"

"That's right."

"Are you going to drive me all around town just so you can spout this nonsense?"

Filippo pressed down hard on the accelerator.

"Slow down," I yelled in fright. "Slow down, you idiot."

He had switched on his brights and was barreling at top speed toward a brick wall surrounding the park named for his father.

"You'll never marry her. Giovanna belongs to me."

I was terrified. I threw my arms up to protect my face, expecting the sound of the crash. Filippo slammed on the brakes at the very last instant, and the sports car screeched to a halt just inches short of the wall.

I staggered out of the car and then grabbed Filippo with fury. I dragged him out of the car, punched him hard, and threw him down onto the asphalt. He didn't even try to defend himself. The harsh yellow light of the streetlamps illuminated his idiotic simpering smile and the blood running out of his nose.

"You're crazy, you need professional help."

"I always take my pills; I'm a good patient."

I was about to haul back and punch him again, but something in his eyes stopped me.

"She'll betray you, just like she did me," he said, wiping the blood off his nose.

He was just a pathetic nut. I told him to go to hell and I started walking back home. When I got there I threw back a couple of really strong gin-and-tonics to quench my fury, and I climbed under the covers, alone, determined to say nothing to Giovanna. Filippo was hoping I would tell her what had happened, so that she'd rush to his side to comfort him. What I thought as I dropped off into slumber was that I should talk to my father about it. That knucklehead, Filippo, might very well cause a scene at the wedding. He was invited, of course. He and his mother would both be given a place of honor at my father's table, along with Prunella, Giovanna's mother. We should alert the Contessa: she would never allow her son to cause an unseemly row; if necessary, she'd make sure he was stuffed with sedatives. Selvaggia loathed Giovanna. She had always cast a jaundiced eye on Filippo's relationship with a Barovier, a young woman branded by her father's disgrace; she also blamed Giovanna for her son's car crash. Of course, she had never said any of this explicitly; that would have been far too vulgar. She hadn't needed to: a couple of venomous remarks had been quite sufficient, casual poisonous darts that Giovanna and her mother had been obliged to receive with smiles on their faces. And on the day of the wedding, they would all feign delight, exchange false hugs, and plant pecks on one another's cheeks. False and hypocritical best-wishes and sincere thank-yous. But that was life in our town. The leading families never caused scenes in public. And that went for Filippo as well.

I summoned the strength to sit up in bed. My head was spinning, but not too badly. I gave up on the idea of an espresso; a cup of hot chamomile tea would do me more good. I dragged myself as far as the kitchen, and that's when the phone rang.

"What are you doing still at home?" my father's voice rapped out over the phone, without so much as a hello.

"I only have a couple of appointments later on this morning."

"You need to make sure the office is up and running anyway. A self-respecting professional—"

"Papa!" I broke in with annoyance. "Last night was my bachelor party, and as if that's not enough, I had an unpleasant run-in with Filippo."

Silence. "I see," he said after a while. "Is Giovanna with you?"

"No."

"Her colleagues from the law office and the secretaries organized a surprise party for her, before the wedding. You know, the sort of thing they do in law firms in Milan. But she didn't show up, and no one knows where she is. They were upset, they wanted to give her presents."

That was typical of Giovanna. She'd vanish from time to time, forgetting to tell other people about it, and with just a few days to go before the wedding, she must be busy taking care of the last few details. She was a real perfectionist, born under Virgo, as she liked to point out.

I walked over to my law office, from my apartment in the center of town. As always, I stopped for a moment in front of my father's law office, and studied the gleaming bronze plaque. Beneath his name—Avvocato Antonio Visentin—stretched the imposing list of his underlings. The fourth name was hers: Giovanna Barovier. Papa had taken her on as an intern, as a favor to me. Like Selvaggia, at first he was opposed to our relationship, but then he had understood that I was in love with her, and that Giovanna was better than her father's soiled reputation. Once we were married, I'd join his law firm too, and there would be a new brass plate on the firm's front door, with my name underneath my father's. Until that day, he wanted me to run my own practice, he wanted me to make ends meet with no help from him. He didn't want anyone to think that he'd made me a partner just because I was his son. It didn't matter that that's exactly what all the other lawyers in the area had done for their sons, without a second thought. Not him. He was the finest, the best-known, the most respected lawyer in town. He often said that the children of the leading families were softies, incapable of running the companies their parents had struggled to build. Even if he had never uttered his name, I knew that he was thinking of Filippo in particular. My father had put me through a tough and demanding apprenticeship. I took my degree in law at the University of Padua, and then I moved to Milan to work as an intern. After that, I opened a law office of my own in town. I struggled to build up my own list of clients, though hardly an impressive one. The most desirable clients, the ones with money, were all his. More than once, I had found myself battling his paralegals and junior lawyers, and Papa was always there, sitting in the audience, to see how I did. I would turn my back to him, but I knew he was there; I could feel his eyes on me. And I always attended his hearings. Papa really was the best. He almost never raised his voice, the way most of the old windbags did who practiced law in our town, but when he stood up and adjusted his lawyer's robes before beginning his summation, a respectful silence would fall over the courtroom; he'd draw that silence out as long as possible, and then he'd break into it with his actorly voice, a voice that all his colleagues envied. My mother used to say that he looked like Jimmy Stewart. Not only physically, and in his gentle and slightly melancholy gaze, but also in his confident, unflappable movements.

Just a week earlier, Papa had made the announcement: I was ready for the big time. At last, he would take me in as a partner. I was deeply moved.

He wrapped his arms around me. "You've done good work, Francesco. You've earned this."

I certainly had earned it. From the day I took my law degree, I'd worked hard to get my name on that plaque; I had specialized in corporate law so that I could become legal counsel to my father's most important client, the Torrefranchi Foundation. The foundation had been created as a cultural entity, but once the Northeast had become the locomotive of the Italian economy, it had been transformed into a formidable consortium of corporations, capable of undertaking ventures in every field of business, and doing deals with anyone. Its unquestioned chief executive was Selvaggia, the Contessa.

Selvaggia had been born into a family of farmers, but she had succeeded in marrying the only aristocrat in the district: the Conte Giannino, who was a couple of decades older than her. Before she was married, her first name was Fausta—her maiden surname was Tonon—but she had promptly changed Fausta to the much more chic name of Selvaggia when the count asked her to marry him. She was canny, and she had a sharp business sense. After her husband died, she invested the money he had left her in successful business operations, bringing most of the area's manufacturers into various partnerships with her. And the legal brains behind it all had always been

Papa. He had made the Contessa's dreams possible, and he had reached out to all those people who could help to shore up the Foundation's image and power at a local level: politicians, artists, intellectuals, judges, and even a few high-ranking men of the cloth.

And that was where I would practice law. After years of hard work, I could finally savor the fruits of success. I'd become a respected lawyer, a powerful man, in town and throughout the region. Just like my father. My life was already planned out, engraved in golden letters. I was a Visentin. And I was about to marry the most beautiful girl in town.

Standing outside the door of my law office was my first client of the day. I had no secretary, so he had waited for me in the street. He was a turkey farmer, heavyset, about sixty years old. He spoke only in dialect. As I was showing him into the office, he explained that near his farm some young people had held a "rave"—he read the word haltingly from a note that his grandson had written out for him—and his turkeys, terrified by the pounding music, had stampeded against their pen, crushing one another in panic. Nearly all the turkeys had been killed. He wanted thirty thousand euros in damages. It was a relatively minor case, and one I was by no means likely to win. Still, you never refuse a paying client without a good reason. After talking it over, we shook hands and the turkey farmer, clearly satisfied, left the office. On his way out, he confided that he had heard good things about me at the tavern.

My second client that morning was a woman I knew from high school. She wanted me to represent her in a divorce case. I knew her husband, too. When we were in boarding school, we had played on the same volleyball team for a few seasons.

"Why don't you ask Giovanna to take your case?" I asked her. "She has more experience in this area."

"My husband has already hired a lawyer from your father's law office."

"Then I'm sorry, I can't help you. When I get back from my honeymoon I'm going to start working there, too."

I recommended that she go to another lawyer, and she congratulated me on my upcoming wedding, unable to conceal a hint of envy.

A short while later, I received a phone call from Carla, Giovanna's best friend and her maid of honor at our wedding.

"I can't find her anywhere," she told me.

"She hasn't even gone into the law office. She must be busy driving the seamstress crazy, or maybe the florist. You know how Giovanna can be."

"We were at the seamstress's shop yesterday," she told me. Then she fell silent for a few moments. Finally, embarrassed and hesitant, she asked if Giovanna had spoken to me.

"About what?"

"I'm not really sure. I only know that it was important. Very important."

"Important how? I don't follow you."

Carla wouldn't say anything more; she hung up with a muttered goodbye. She had recently moved back to town after a long period living and working in southern Italy, in Campania. She had taken her college degree in biology, and had moved to Caserta with a classmate from the university. Then he broke up with her, and Giovanna had helped Carla find a job back in town, at the local health board. At least, that's what my fiancée had told me. I didn't know Carla very well. I knew that Giovanna and Carla had been close friends since they were little girls, and had stayed in touch ever since. I had never had such a close friend. I knew everyone in town, I spent lots of time at the country club and the café in the town piazza when it was time for aperitifs. I chatted about this and that with lots of different people, I went to parties, but I was a Visentin, in some sense on a higher, unattainable plane from ordinary people. Even as a child, I had lived with a sense of privilege, which had always obliged other people—young and old—to think of me as different from them. Back then, there was none of the widespread prosperity of the present day; social distinctions were more sharply drawn. Still, though, even now that lots of people own villas with extensive grounds and beautiful swimming pools and drive Mercedes, BMWs, and Ferraris, I continue to sense that time-honored respect for my family. My mother had done her best to persuade me to become best friends with Filippo, but we'd never liked each other much, even when we were still in short pants. I'd met lots and lots of other boys like him at the boarding school where I lived for the five years of high school. I'd had a good time, but I'd never really established any solid friendships. Things were different at university, but by then it was too late. I realized that I was no longer open to or interested in anything deeper than a passing acquaintance. I divided the world into the likable and the obnoxious. It was the same with girls. I had had plenty of girls, and I had no special memories of my time with them. Sex, affection, a certain period of fun and enjoyment, and then a tactful conclusion, no hard feelings, as my social position required. Then I met Giovanna and everything changed. With her I had plunged into an ocean of feelings and sensations that I was unable to understand in rational terms. Giovanna was my woman, my lover, and my best friend. She was my whole life. And I was happy in a way that I had not experienced since my mother died. Everything seemed perfect. My world, my future.

I walked home, pulled my car out of the garage, and drove over to Giovanna's house. It was foggy, as usual.

My fiancée lived in a little town house on the outskirts of town. When we got back from our honeymoon, she would come to live with me. My house was a perfect modernist architectural gem, carved out of a venerable old 2,500-square-foot building. My father had spent a fortune to restore the original wooden roof beams that ran the length of the ceiling, and to uncover sections of wall built by Venetian masons in the sixteenth century. Her house, in contrast, was comfortable and attractive, but otherwise unremarkable. And I liked living in the center of town, just a short walk from the piazza, in the heart of town, where things were hopping. Where everything was just a short walk away.

Giovanna's red Mazda was parked in the yard. As I got out, I noticed that her wheels were caked with mud. I shook my head and smiled. Giovanna loved to drive out into the countryside, where she bought salamis and fresh eggs from farmers she knew. And she had put together a sizable network of suppliers for fresh farm products.

I rang the bell, but there was no answer. I pulled my set of keys out of my overcoat pocket and unlocked the door.

"Giovanna, my love! Where are you?"

The house was silent. I continued calling her name. I climbed up the stairs that led to the bedroom.

I walked over to the big canopy bed, and drew the curtains aside, but it was empty. Then I walked into the bathroom. The first thing I saw was her leg, dangling over the side of the bathtub.

I took three urgent steps, and looked down into her wide-open eyes, staring at me through the still water.

"Giovanna," I whispered.

"Giovanna!" I shouted, an instant later.

I cradled her in my arms until the ambulance arrived. Expert hands took her away from me; I stood watching, awaiting a verdict that came as no surprise.

"I'm sorry, the patient is dead."

I nodded without speaking, numb, inert.

A medical technician helped me take off my overcoat and jacket, both drenched with bathwater, and guided me gently downstairs.

From the living room, I could hear a voice calling the Carabinieri.

Three of them arrived a little later. Sergeant Mele and two young Carabinieri I had never seen before. I had known the inspector all my life. He arrived in town with the rank of corporal and then he had worked his way up, spending the rest of his career here. He walked over to the sofa where I was sitting and placed a hand firmly on my shoulder. I felt his fingers squeeze my shoulder.

"I'm sorry," he said, in a low voice.

Then he climbed the stairs. He came back a few minutes later. With a fatherly tone of voice, he pulled words out of me one by one, but it was painful to relive the experience of discovering Giovanna's corpse.

"I have to call the investigating magistrate and the medical examiner so they can take a look at things. You know how these things work."

Sure, I knew, and I didn't say a word. Giovanna was dead. Then and there, I didn't care much how it had happened. It could have been an aneurysm, a heart attack. What did it matter? Giovanna was gone. Mele went out into the yard to make his phone calls. It couldn't have been later than two in the afternoon, but it was practically dark already, the fog had gotten heavier and had turned ash grey.

My father came running into the room. He saw me and hurled himself against me, his arms wrapped tight around me, his chest heaving with sobs. I thought to myself that the last time I'd seen him like this was at my mother's funeral.

"How awful, Francesco. I can't believe it."

"Take him home," Mele told him, draping over my shoulders a blanket he had picked up from an easy chair. Giovanna's scent wafted up from the cover; I hugged it to my body like a second skin. It was her favorite blanket. In the winter, she'd curl up in her armchair, wrapped in that sky-blue cashmere blanket.

Papa helped me into his Jaguar. "I'll take you to the villa."

"No. I want to go home. I need to be alone."

Outside of my house, he held one of my hands in both of his. "I'm sorry your mother can't be here right now. She would have known the words to comfort you."

My mother. The most important women in my life were both dead. I was crushed by a collapsing wall of grief. I wished I could pass out, plunge into unconsciousness, but I felt strangely lucid.

"Can you tell Prunella?" I asked.

"Of course. I'll do it right away."

Prunella, the "white widow"—slang for a woman whose husband was far, far away, and as good as dead. She'd already lost her husband, and now she'd lost her daughter and only child.

Her family had been the most important family in town until her husband, Alvise, had managed to squander a fortune playing roulette in the casinos of Slovenia and Croatia. Two hours by car. He'd leave the house after dinner and return home the next morning, coming back a little poorer from each trip. Until he wound up in prison on arson charges, for having set fire to his own factory. He had hoped to use the money from the insurance to pay off his debts with the banks. It might have worked out, too, if the fire hadn't killed the night watchman, his wife, and their baby girl. After he served his time in prison, he vanished, and no one knew where he had fled. Prunella was left alone, to raise Giovanna. In town, she was known as the widow Barovier. To everyone in town, Alvise was dead.

Prunella, who had once been an arrogant snob, took refuge in religion, her sole comfort against her grief and shame at her loss of social standing.

She was a good woman.

I took Giovanna's blanket off my shoulders and carefully

folded it. Then I took off my clothes and dried myself with a towel. I had just put on a fresh change of clothes when I heard a knock at the door.

It was Don Piero. Good old Don Piero. He was eighty years old, but as chipper and vigorous as always. He had retired years ago, but he'd never abandoned the rectory, where he lived with his elderly housekeeper, who was only a few years younger than him. The new parish priest, a blond Croatian who had tried without success to speak in dialect to bridge the distance with his parishioners, had been obliged to settle for a little apartment in the church hall. Don Piero was still the uncontested master of the souls of the town, and so he would remain until the day he died. There was no bishop persuasive enough to jolly him into a nursing home.

He leveled his dark eyes at me, looking directly into my own. He patted my face with a rough hand, and sank down onto a chair.

"The good Lord has decided to test you, Francesco," he began in pure dialect. "And he's testing the heart of this old priest, too. Poor Giovanna, she was unlucky in life. I had hoped that you could bring her a little peace, but the Lord decided differently. He took her away from us. He decided to gather her to His side. We understand this, isn't that true?"

Don Piero took in the grief and incredulity in my eyes. "Only God can help you through this moment. Surrender to His love, Francesco. Otherwise this grief will become intolerable."

He stood up and headed for the door. Then he thought of something and turned back toward me. "You, Giovanna, and Filippo. You've always had more than the others, but the Lord has reserved a painful existence for all three of you. You know how often I've prayed for you? Your curse is that you are only children. Families as important as yours cannot be entrusted to a single heir; that's tempting fate. I told your parents time and again, but they refused to listen."

He walked back toward me, gave me a kiss on the forehead, and sketched a benediction with his fingers. Then he left without saying goodbye.

The subject of children was a tough one for Giovanna, too. I had always assumed she wanted children. But during our pre-marriage counseling, she had told Don Ante, the Croatian priest, that she did not want to become a mother at that point in her life.

"I'm only thirty," she had told him. "If I become a mother now, it would mean giving up my career."

The parish priest had done his best to change her mind. I said nothing. I was certain that once we were married she would see things differently.

We told Don Ante that we were refraining from full sexual relations, and he pretended to believe us. Then he had launched into a tirade against contraceptives. It was obvious that he came from a backward religious culture, and that he had not yet grasped how things worked in the Northeast. His church was always crowded on Sunday and the offerings were sufficient to provide him with a more-than-adequate living, but the faithful, on certain matters, simply used their own common sense. Giovanna took the pill.

Something distracted me from this line of thought. It was the silence. A silence so intense that I found myself listening to it, experiencing it. I found Giovanna in that silence, and I understood that between the two of us, there could only be the silence of absence. A wave of despair suddenly washed over me. I thought about death. I thought of my own death as a way out. I thought that not a word of what Don Piero had told me made any sense. The grief became physical, a pressure on my chest, making it hard to catch my breath. And still I felt a need to suffer more and more. It seemed to me that my despair was too little in the face of the enormity of the loss of Giovanna. These thoughts came to me in a procession of apparent lucidity. In reality, that silence was deafening, I was plunging into a maelstrom of confusion. Giovanna was dead. She was really, really dead. I would accompany her body to the cemetery. A coffin, a loculus, a marble slab, the letters in gilt metal: first name, last name, date of birth, date of death. And silence, a vast ocean of silence.

The chiming of the church tower clock told me that it was already eleven o'clock, and I was still seated in the same position. My bladder was about to burst, but the idea of going to the bathroom struck me as intolerable just then. Someone rang the doorbell twice. "Papa," I thought to myself. Instead, it was Inspector Mele. His face was lined with weariness and tension.

"I have to take you in to the Carabinieri barracks. The prosecutor has a couple of questions to ask you."

"At this time of night?"

He nodded with an imperceptible movement of his head. "Your father has already been informed."

I hurried into the bathroom. As I was emptying my bladder, I thought about how odd this summons was; I persuaded myself that it must have been the result of an excess of zeal because of the involvement of a Visentin. I followed in my own car behind the vehicle of the Carabinieri all the way to the barracks, a squat building protected by high walls and gates, video cameras, and bulletproof glass. In the late seventies, a terrorist group had planted a bomb, and since then it had been converted into a small fortress.

In Mele's office, the prosecutor, Zan, was seated behind the desk. He was a tall thin man. He was dressed like an American university professor, at least the ones we see in the movies. Tweed jackets with patches on the elbows, loose trousers over the skinny, age-wizened hips, an anonymous tie knotted around the collar of a flannel shirt.

He stood up, grasped my hand, and gestured for me to sit

down. Like Mele, the prosecutor was tense. I was about to ask him why when my father walked in.

"I certainly hope that there is a sound justification for this summons," he said, resting his hands on my shoulders in an affectionate gesture.

"Counselor, be seated," Mele broke in.

Zan ran his hand over his face. "We have requested your presence, counselor," he explained to my father, "entirely in consideration of and respect for your reputation. I am obliged by circumstances to put certain questions to your son pertaining to the death of Giovanna Barovier, and I deemed it to be my duty to inform you of that fact."

My father nodded his head with a smile, acknowledging the collegiality of the gesture. "It strikes me that the urgent nature of these questions imply a development, something of which we would appreciate being informed before responding," he replied in the purest lawyerly language.

Zan looked hard at me. I could feel the sergeant's eyes on me as well.

"Giovanna Barovier was murdered."

"What?" I shouted.

"Do you realize the gravity of such a statement?" my father inquired.

Zan held up both hands in a signal of reassurance. "The preliminary results of the autopsy are unequivocal," he explained. "A hematoma on her sternum clearly demonstrates that she was forcibly held underwater."

"By whom?" I asked.

"That we do not know," Mele responded. "That's why we have to ask you some questions."

I looked at my father. He was clearly thinking the same thing. They were trying to determine if I was the killer. This is what always happens in this kind of investigation. They start with the people who were closest to the victim. Statistically, it was usually one of them. But not in my case. I hadn't killed Giovanna.

"When did you last see the victim?" asked Zan.

The victim. Giovanna had become the victim. Until last night, she'd been my whole life. Now she was the corpse of a murdered woman. The subject of an investigation.

"How was she killed?" I asked.

The prosecutor shifted uneasily in his chair, glancing at my father in search of assistance. Papa took one of my hands in both of his. "Answer his question, if you feel that you can; otherwise the prosecutor will understand, and we'll come back some other time."

I drew a deep breath. "Yesterday morning," I answered robotically. "Giovanna slept at my house. We ate breakfast together, and then she left."

"And you didn't see her again after that?"

"No."

"Are you certain that you didn't go to her house last night?"

"My son already answered that question," my father broke in.

Zan seemed increasingly uncomfortable. This time he looked over at the inspector.

"We need to know where you were between 1 and 3 A.M.," Mele said, brusquely.

So that's when Giovanna had been murdered. But what was she doing in the bathtub at that time of night?

"I was at the Club Diana, for my bachelor party. Then I left the club, and I ran into Filippo Calchi Renier. I think I got back to my house just a little before 3 A.M."

My father shot me a disappointed look. It hadn't been a very smart answer. But I didn't give a damn. I hadn't killed Giovanna. I wanted to shout that out with all my strength, but I couldn't. No one had accused me of anything yet.

"A little before three," the inspector considered the answer out loud. "I guess, at that hour, no one saw you come home."

"No one, as far as I can remember."

"Did Giovanna try to call you during the day?"

"We spoke on the phone a couple of times. She asked me for advice about a couple of details concerning our wedding plans."

Zan cleared his throat, signaling that it was Mele's turn to take over the questioning.

"Did Giovanna Barovier ever tell you that she needed to talk to you about a very important matter?"

"No."

"A witness informs us to that effect, with absolute certainty, claiming to have learned it directly from your fiancée."

"I can't imagine what you're talking about."

"The witness told us that Giovanna wanted to inform you of a relationship she was having with another man. A relationship that had been going on for quite a while," the prosecutor blurted out hastily.

"That's not true," I mumbled.

"We're checking into it," Zan drove the point home. "But now you must certainly understand why we need to establish with precision exactly what you did and where you were during the hours in which the murder was committed."

"No. We don't understand at all," my father broke in harshly. "You're treating my son as a suspect, not a witness. If you have any specific accusations to make, please do so. Otherwise, this interview is over."

"We are in the middle of an investigation," Zan mumbled. "We are only interested in clearing up a few key points so that we can move forward as quickly as possible. You know as well as we do that, in cases of this sort, time is of the essence."

My father stood up. "Let's go, Francesco."

"Hold on," said Mele. "The prosecutor is right, and anyway, there is evidence that requires us to check out Francesco's alibi."

"Well, at least that's some straight talk," I snapped out sarcastically.

The inspector looked me right in the eyes. "Giovanna engaged in a sex act just before she was murdered. Either it was with you, or else it's true that she had a lover."

I felt the blood drain from my face. "She must have been raped," I whispered.

Mele shook his head. "The sex was consensual," he explained. "We are asking you—and we are required to do so—whether by any chance Giovanna confessed to you that she had a lover, or whether you discovered somehow that she had a lover. If so, before returning home, did you go to see her, argue with her, and shove her head underwater in a fit of temporary insanity?"

"A state of frenzy," Zan specified.

"You have the wrong person," I said in a faint voice.

"That's probably true," Mele replied. "But we need answers."

I made a tremendous effort to control myself. All I wanted was to leave that office and be left alone. "I did not have sex with Giovanna, I knew nothing about any lover. Can I go now?"

"There are still a few questions I'd like to ask," said Zan.

My father said only: "No."

"All right," Zan agreed. "We'll verify your son's statement against a DNA examination of the semen found in the victim's body, and against the statements of the other witnesses."

"My son will not allow himself to be subjected to any comparative testing," my father intoned angrily.

"There's no need, counselor," Mele pointed out. "Francesco spent time in that house, and we have lots of samples at our disposal, his razor, his toothbrush . . ."

We left without saying goodbye. I walked briskly toward my car.

"Francesco!"

"I want to be alone, Papa."

I was so upset that I couldn't manage to find my car key. I left the car parked in the plaza outside the barracks and returned home on foot. The bracing chill in the air helped to clear my head. Giovanna had a lover. Who? How long had this affair been going on? If they hadn't told me about the sperm, I never would have believed it. One thing I knew for sure: he was the murderer. But Mele and Zan suspected me. I had no respect for the prosecutor, a view of him that was widely shared in the courts. Zan had chosen a career as a prosecutor once he realized that he was not going to be successful as a lawyer. He was, however, very careful not to make enemies among the powerful and influential, and his obsequious attitude toward my father was clear evidence of that. Mele was another matter. He was a classic public servant. If it had been up to him, my father would have been told to wait in the hall while they questioned me behind closed doors. But he was an honest and conscientious person, and I felt sure that I could rely upon him.

When I finally made it back home, I poured myself a large cognac and threw it back, without even taking off my overcoat. Then I walked from room to room, gathering up all the pictures of Giovanna, and I threw them into the trash.

"That's where you belong, you slut."

I had to wait for a sullen, unprecedented fury to wash out of my mind and body. Then I broke into sobs, pulled the photographs out of the trash can, and hugged them to my chest.

"How could you do this to me, Giovanna? What happened to you, my love?"

* * *

He boarded the first morning train. He had hidden his duffel bag in a nearby field. It would only be a burden, a hindrance to him in what he had to do next. The train cars were full of dozing commuters; no one paid him the slightest attention. He stepped off the train at the first stop, a few miles away but already in a different province. He ate breakfast at the train station coffee bar. Two officers of the Polfer, or railroad police, came in and ordered yet another of the succession of espressos they'd drink that day; one of the two officers gazed at the man thoughtfully, observing him as if the face reminded him of someone. It gave the man a sharp stab of pain in his belly. It was a stab of fear. If they had asked him for ID, that would have spelled the end of his plan. He couldn't allow that to happen. He kept a sidelong eye on the policeman in the big plate-glass mirror behind the bar. The police officer, a stout fifty-year-old with white hair tufting out from beneath his hat, had been momentarily distracted by the female barista. She wanted to know about a gang of Gypsies that had been sighted in the area over the past few days. The man heaved a sigh of relief. He turned his gaze to his own reflection in the mirror. His hair was too long, too tangled. In fact, in those parts men his age, men with jobs and families, went to the barbershop more frequently than he did. He left a couple of ten-cent coins on the counter for a tip, and left the coffee bar. He went to the public bathrooms at the far end of the train station, and used a rubber band to tie his hair back in a ponytail. Then he headed into town. He stepped into a phone booth and dialed the number again. Again, he heard the anonymous and impersonal voice of the answering machine. The man didn't know what to make of it. Angry and disappointed, he positioned himself on a bench near the town church. He didn't have long to wait. An old man pedaled up on a bicycle, leaned it against the wall by the church's main portal, and went in, without locking the bike. He wouldn't be inside for very long, just time enough for a prayer and a genuflection. But the man would already be long gone. He swung onto the bicycle seat and pedaled away quickly, thinking to himself as he rode that, around there, certain customs would never vanish. As for himself, he'd never been a regular church-goer, and lately he'd stopped going entirely. In his own life, he'd always found more spiritual comfort and understanding in the arms of a skilled whore than kneeling at a confessional.

The dense fog was thinning, as punctual as death that time of the year. He would need to find a place to hide, and there was no time to waste. Last night he had slept in a shed on a construction site; he had almost frozen to death.

He pedaled for ten or fifteen miles. He still remembered how to use the gears properly and, despite his age, his muscles still had their spring.

He felt like clipping a playing card to the front fork, so that he could listen to the tack-a-tack-a-tack in the spinning spokes, a sound that seemed to belong to a lost, archaic world, confusingly enveloped in another kind of fog, the fog of memory. When he reached the outskirts of town, he stopped outside a grocery store. He peered in through the plate glass window and saw that both the owner and the few customers were third-world immigrants. Reassured, he walked into the store with a confident step, smiled genially, and began to pull canned goods and other items from the shelves. When his shopping basket was full, he walked over to the cash register.

"Two bottles of red wine," he asked.

"No wine. No alcohol," the proprietor replied in foreign-accented Italian.

He slid the two plastic bags filled with groceries onto the handlebars, and pedaled back out into the countryside. The fog almost made him miss the dirt road he was looking for. He was obliged to make a wide circle back before he could turn into the lane. As he rode along between skeletal grape vines, the fog grew even denser. The rough surface of the road made the bicycle rattle and jolt; it wasn't easy to keep his balance. He was beginning to feel tired; he needed to rest and think about everything that had happened since his arrival the day before.

He rode practically blind for a couple of miles, until he could finally make out the silhouette of a house through the fog. He dismounted and wheeled the bicycle, careful to make no noise over the last fifty yards.

The house was shrouded in silence. He circled cautiously around it until he realized that the building was completely abandoned. Reassured, he peered in through one of the windows, whose shutters dangled slightly askew, each from a single surviving hinge. He shattered the window glass with an elbow to get inside. When he set foot on the floor, he felt fragments of glass crunch and snap beneath the soles of his hiking boots. He ran his fingers along the wall until he felt a light switch. He flipped it on: there was no power. Making his way by the flame of a lighter, he managed to find the kitchen. It was empty, except for a table with a broken marble top. He rummaged through the drawers and, amidst the clutter of mismatched cutlery, wine corks, multicolored rubber bands, and rusted corkscrews, he found several candle ends.

By the light of the candle flames, he saw that he had stumbled into an eighteenth-century mansion, abandoned for years, probably because of some never-resolved dispute over an estate. Aside from a few skittering mice and a dropped ceiling of spiderwebs, there were no signs of life. The furniture had all been taken away, except for a pile of chairs in the dining room and a swaybacked sofa. The chairs were decorated with finely crafted intarsia work, but they were badly worm-eaten. In the middle of the back wall stood an enormous and empty fireplace. It was brutally cold. He managed to kick a couple of chairs to pieces, and he piled up the shattered wood in the fireplace. It was almost dark by now; no one would notice the smoke. He had a nice fire going before long. Later, he would retrieve the duffel bag containing his possessions. The man pulled the sofa closer to the flames and sat huddled, still wrapped in his heavy jacket. He made himself a sandwich with a can of tunafish, and opened a can of Mecca Cola. He pulled a transistor radio out of his jacket pocket and switched it on. He tuned the radio to a local station that broadcast only Italian music requested by listeners; the callers all spoke dialect, as did the announcer. After an old hit by the pop singer Drupi dedicated to a certain Rosi, the DJ, Franchino, took a call from an elderly female caller.

"Ciao, Franchino, it's me, Maria," she introduced herself.

"*Carissima*, it's been a while since we've heard your voice."

"Eh, I'm so busy with my grandchildren. There's four of them now, and you know, at my age . . ."

"Oh, come on, you're practically a teenager. So, Maria, what song would you like to request?"

"'Tears in the Wind' by Adamo. And I want to dedicate it to that girl that died the other night, Giovanna Barovier. Poor girl, to think that she was getting married next week. It makes me think about my poor sister . . ."

"Yes, we mentioned it during the news report at the top of the hour," Franchino interrupted her. "A sad story."

The man switched off the radio. He'd heard enough.

* * *

"Answer the test questions by selecting the number of minutes of foreplay that women say they like, depending on the setting: 'Sex in the bathroom during a party?'" Rocco read out loud from the latest issue of the Italian edition of *Men's Health,* holding it up to the dome light in the Jeep Cherokee.

"Three minutes," answered Denis.

"Sex on a first date?"

"Half an hour."

"Yeah, okay . . . Sex in her parents' house?"

"Ten minutes, better not to waste time, or else . . ."

Rocco marked each of Denis's answers with a check mark on the test. They were both sitting in the back seat while Lucio, in the driver's seat, prepared three abundant lines of cocaine, using a circular hand mirror as a surface.

They had been parked for two hours now, waiting for the bluish light from the television set in the little villa finally turned off.

"Christ, this is a drag," said Denis, "if you ask me, the old lady's fallen asleep watching 'The Costanzo Show.'"

"'The Costanzo Show' isn't on the air anymore," Rocco replied, as he added up his friend's test score.

"Well, okay, then she tossed back a couple of shots of Vov liqueur and nodded off on the sofa, and now she's overdosed."

"Here, take this and shut up," Lucio ordered, handing over the hand mirror with the lines of coke.

Denis snorted the line with a straw from his Coke.

"Nice fucking technique, way to snort," Rocco commented, with the air of an offended purist.

"TV's off," Lucio reported, while Rocco clamped his left nostril shut.

"Let's get moving," Denis suggested impatiently.

"No. Give her the time to have a piss, and then we'll catch her in bed."

"Fuck that, let's catch her on the toilet," Rocco snickered.

"That's disgusting," commented Denis. "By the way, why do we always have to hit on stinking old women, never a nice piece of young pussy?"

"Lucio keeps those for himself . . ." Rocco said, with a mischievous smile.

Lucio turned sharply, staring menacingly back over his shoulder at Rocco: "What's that supposed to mean?"

"You know what I mean."

"I don't know fuck."

"Oh yeah? Then why wouldn't you let us inflict a little punishment on that sweet piece of pussy, the Barovier? A girl like that driving around alone at night is just looking for hard cock. And she got what she was looking for. And that's not all she got. You wouldn't have had anything to do with that, by any chance, would you?"

Lucio turned to stare at the dark windows of the little villa. Then his arm shot back, a sharp blow of the elbow to Rocco's nose, followed by a spurt of blood. He sat tensely, his elbow poised to strike again. But Rocco was too busy moaning, covering his nose with both hands, like a Hindu rapt in prayer.

"Shit, you knocked over the mirror," was all Denis had to say, bent over in a frantic attempt to sniff up whatever cocaine he could glean from the carpet.

Lucio opened the car door and got out, circling around the Jeep and opening the rear compartment. He reached in and pulled out a baseball bat, then pulled Rocco's door open. He jerked Rocco out of the car and kicked him in the balls, forcing him into a kneeling position on the ground before him. He raised the baseball hat high into the air over Rocco's head. Rocco continued to snivel over his poor bleeding nose.

"Lucio, what the fuck do you think you're doing!" Denis had finally decided to get out of the Cherokee and say something, though he remained at a respectful distance from the baseball bat. "Don't do it; what did he do to you?"

Lucio stared down at Rocco, unsure what to do next:

"Don't you ever dare. Never again. Ever."

Rocco managed to nod with a whimper.

Lucio lowered the bat; he clearly considered the matter settled.

He turned to Denis: "Let's go, the old lady must be asleep by now." He pulled his ski mask over his head.

As she lay stretched out on the floor, gagged and bound, her eyes burning from the fluoroacetophenone spray, her heart racing crazily, the old woman would remember a cascade of objects, dresser drawers, clothing, and the athletic shoes of her attackers as they stepped over her, on her, and every so often, kicked her in what was clearly an intentional infliction of pain.

For the Cherokee Gang, as they had all too predictably decided to call themselves, this was their sixth home invasion and robbery. They all employed the same technique: take the victim by surprise, in her sleep, usually an old woman living alone, then tie her up and gag her. And then turn the house inside out, destroying anything they couldn't take with them. It was Denis's job to blind the victim momentarily with an anti-mugger spray. That had been Lucio's idea. He had a twisted sense of humor about these things. Rocco was assigned to finding objects of value and Lucio went to work with his baseball bat.

On the desk of Inspector Mele, the file on the gang got thicker with each home invasion, but there were no clues at all. He figured they were a group of drug addicts from out of town.

* * *

My father arrived at my house at seven in the morning, and the phone began ringing at eight o'clock sharp. Reporters. They had caught the scent of the scoop of the year and they were churning the water, in a feeding frenzy, in search of a statement. Papa had shown me the front page of the two local papers. They reported the news of my fiancée's death, with the old version, from accidental causes. Then they had seized on the troubled past of Alvise Barovier, Giovanna's father. I wasted no time reading any of the articles. Each time the phone rang, my father picked up the receiver and identified himself, and each time the reporters became a little less frenzied and aggressive at the mention of his name. The word "murder" was in the air, and became gradually more frequent.

"How did Prunella take it?" I asked him.

"Poor woman. She's a wreck. After the end of her marriage, Giovanna was everything to her."

"She was everything to me, too," I remarked, bitterly. "I wonder if she 'was everything' to her lover."

Papa shook his head. "I still can't believe it. But didn't you notice anything was wrong?"

"I'm afraid not. Otherwise she'd still be alive."

Shortly after eleven, Mele showed up. "There's a problem," he announced. "I need you to come to the barracks." He turned and addressed my father as well. "The prosecutor would appreciate it if you would come, too."

This time, Zan came right to the point. "Filippo Calchi Renier claims he never left his house."

He's crazy, for real, I thought.

"Unless you can suggest some other witness, you have no alibi after two in the morning," the prosecutor added. "The other witnesses who were present at the Club Diana confirm that you were there until 2 A.M."

"Filippo is lying," I said.

"And why on earth would he want to lie?" asked Zan.

I said nothing. If I began to explain that we had quarreled over Giovanna, I would only make them more suspicious.

"Maybe the witness is confused," my father put in cautiously.

"Maybe," Zan said.

"Do you intend to name Francesco as a person of interest?"

The prosecutor hastened to reassure Papa. "No, no. We're only anxious to eliminate all doubts about your son's legal standing."

I was sick and tired of playing these petty games. "Are you investigating other leads, though?" I asked in a cutting tone.

"Yes," Mele replied laconically.

Zan adjusted his glasses nervously on the bridge of his nose. "The problem is, this is a complicated case. There are no witnesses, and the body wasn't discovered until hours after the murder took place."

"In other words, all you have is the killer's sperm," I broke in.

Mele and Zan looked at one another, and said nothing.

My father walked me out of the prosecutor's office, and over to the café in the main piazza for an espresso. On our way over, a number of people stopped us to express their condolences. I would have preferred to stay shut up at home, but Papa was implacable: I had to show myself in public and display my grief and my innocence. As we left the café, we encountered a news crew from Antenna N/E, the leading broadcaster in the area. Directing the news crew was Adalberto Beggiolin, a two-bit reporter who was completely devoid of professional ethics. I saw him every morning at court, with a microphone in one hand and a cameraman at his heels, trolling every courtroom where a trial was in progress. All he needed was a minor purse snatching to put together a three-minute report. Beggiolin supplied the news that the town wanted to hear.

"Can I ask you a few questions?" he asked, cautiously.

"Certainly," Papa replied on my behalf.

The cameraman lifted his equipment to his shoulder, and as if by magic, a small cluster of rubberneckers assembled.

"We now know for certain that your fiancée, Giovanna Barovier, was murdered," he said, in a booming voice. For a moment he looked around, enjoying the effect his statement produced. "Is it true that the investigators questioned you at length?"

I looked sidewise at my father's face. He hadn't reacted a bit, and looked as confident as always.

I tried to imitate his poker face. "I'm sad to say that it's true: Giovanna was murdered. It is also true that I was questioned on two separate occasions, and I am doing my best to help the investigators in any way I can."

"Do you suspect anyone in particular?" the reporter drilled in.

"No. No one."

"Do you think that the murder has anything to do with Alvise Barovier's troubles with the law?"

"I doubt it. That's an old piece of history, from fifteen years back."

"Doesn't it strike you as odd that your fiancée would be taking a bath at that time of the night? And how did the murderer get into the house? There are no signs of breaking and entering on doors or windows. I checked for myself."

Within a few hours, the whole town would be wondering the same thing, and then everyone would learn about the seminal fluid. Francesco Visentin—a cuckold even before he could become a husband. I wanted to turn on my heel and walk away, but everyone was staring at me.

"I see that you know more about this matter than I do," I complimented the journalist. "To tell the truth, I can't answer your questions. I hope the investigators provide some answers soon."

Beggiolin wasn't satisfied. I could see it from the grimace of disappointment framed by his fashionable little goatee. "Giovanna let the murderer into her house; how many people could have expected access to her home in the middle of the night?"

He had painted me into a corner. Luckily my father intervened. He stood in front of the television camera, staring into the lens. "Our family is suffering immense pain right now. We ask that you respect our grief and our loss. Now it's up to the investigators, who have our complete trust, to identify and arrest Giovanna's killer."

Theatrically, he shook Beggiolin's hand, thanking him for the service he had rendered to the community, then he took me by the arm and we walked off, followed by the buzz of excited comments.

"I told you it was a bad idea to come to the piazza café for an espresso."

"No. This is something we needed to do," Papa whispered. "You have to get used to journalists and to gossip. Just never forget who you are, and everything will turn out fine."

I shook off his arm and stepped away. "No, I don't know who I am anymore," I blurted. "In just one week I was supposed to marry Giovanna, but now she's dead, and the man who killed her was her lover. You tell me who I am."

"Lower your voice," he warned. "You're a Visentin, you'll always be a Visentin. What matters now is getting you out of this mess with as little damage as possible."

"What about Giovanna? Don't you care about finding her killer?"

"More than anything else on earth," he answered in a firm voice. "But we must take care to avoid being overwhelmed by the situation. Giovanna was cheating on you, her family's unsavory past will come back to the surface. Everyone will be talking about us, and we have to go on living in this town."

I wrapped my arms around him. "I can't take it, Papa."

"Buck up. I'm here, and I'll never abandon you."

I walked with him to the front door of his law office, then I went back home. I was rummaging in my pocket for the keys when I heard the unmistakable sound of a bicycle rattling along under the porticoes. In our town, bicycles are one of the most common means of transportation, and you learn from the earliest age to recognize all the variations on the sounds they make. I turned around. It was Carla. She was heading straight toward me. The bicycle was brand-new, and made in China. It was a copy of an old Italian Bianchi: a girl's bike, black with gold trim and old-fashioned rod brakes. The front wheel grazed the tips of my shoes.

"Who killed Giovanna?" she demanded in a broken voice.

Her cheeks were red from the cold, her eyes swollen with weeping. She was clearly upset, on the verge of a nervous breakdown.

"Come inside."

"No. I want to know who killed her."

"I don't know."

"Was it you?"

"Don't be ridiculous."

"Maybe she confessed that she had a lover and you couldn't take it."

So that's who the mysterious witness was who had told the police all about Giovanna's lover. I should have guessed. Carla and Giovanna were lifelong friends.

"Come inside, please. I need to know everything."

"I don't trust you," she hissed.

I spread my arms in desolation. "Do you think I want to hurt you in some way? Don't you understand that she was killed by her lover? Do you know who he was? What did Giovanna tell you about him?"

She opened her purse and pulled out a rumpled pack of cigarettes. She took one out and clamped it between her lips. Giovanna had been a smoker too.

I hadn't smoked since I was at university and I couldn't stand it when Giovanna smoked in the house or, worse, in the car. But I never said anything. I didn't want to come off as the typical preachy ex-smoker, but most of all, I liked the smell and taste of the tobacco in her mouth when I kissed her. I would let my tongue wander over hers and then over her teeth and palate. I wondered if her lover liked that taste too. I felt a shiver run down my back. How many aspects of Giovanna had I shared with her killer?

Carla lit the cigarette and sucked hungrily at the smoke. "She told me about her lover the other morning. We were at the seamstress's shop, trying her wedding dress for the final fitting. She was a wreck; she told me that she had decided to confess everything to you."

"That's all? She didn't tell you anything else?"

Carla stared at me for a long time. She was uncertain whether or not to trust me. She dropped her cigarette butt on the ground and crushed it out with the heel of her shoe.

"She told me that she had become the slut of the man who had ruined her life. Those were her exact words."

I stood there, petrified. I mulled those words over in my mind, in search of a possible meaning. But I couldn't figure one out. They were only terrifying. Giovanna must have been in a state of complete despair to describe herself with such contempt.

"You don't know anything else?"

Carla mounted her bicycle. "What about you? How much do you know?"

I watched as she pedaled away beneath the portico and then vanished around a curve.

On the evening news show, Beggiolin outdid himself. He managed to create an aura of mystery around the murder that would lure the television audience into watching Antenna N/E news until the case was fully resolved. Even though he didn't say so explicitly, it was clear that the investigators were trying to establish my guilt or innocence.

I was unable to eat. I drained a couple of glasses of cognac and I knocked back a couple of sleeping pills on top of them. They were Giovanna's sleeping pills. She frequently suffered from insomnia. I had always blamed her problems getting to sleep on the stress of her job and the tension of preparing for the wedding. But in reality, the reason that Giovanna couldn't fall asleep was that she had become the slut of the man who had ruined her life. That phrase was stuck in my mind, driven in like a nail by a hammer, and when it came to the surface it caused a dull pain that left me panting and breathless.

I dropped off into a heavy slumber. In the morning I woke up stunned and confused. My tongue felt like a block of wood in my mouth. I took a shower and stepped out to buy the morning newspapers. The vendor looked at me with a diffident curiosity. My father was right: I would have to get used to suspicion and gossip.

Back at home I made another cup of coffee and began reading. The dailies had nothing more than what Beggiolin had already said on the news. But they had done interview after interview with ordinary people, from an elementary school teacher to a supermarket cashier. In the absence of any solid, fresh news, they had seized on her father's past, asking the man in the street what he thought about how that old story had affected poor Giovanna Barovier. There were also a number of articles about me, but I wasted no time reading them. I put on my overcoat and left the house. The time had come to face Prunella's pain and grief.

Prunella still lived in the villa that Alvise had built at the end of the sixties, one of the nicest homes in town, though with the passage of time it was slowly collapsing into ruin.

The front gate was open. The expansive garden was still in good condition. Prunella herself did the gardening. A woman whom I had never seen before opened the door when I knocked. She greeted me courteously and led me into the living room. There were a number of people seated on the old sofas, upholstered in leather that was worn but still shiny and presentable. They were all holding hands and praying. Prunella greeted me with a nod and continued praying with unabated fervor. A man who looked to be about forty invited me to join the group but I shook my head no. I left the living room and waited in an adjoining room. Prunella came in a few minutes later.

"They're my friends from our prayer group," she explained. "They've come to comfort me."

She spread her arms in a gesture that struck me as excessive and theatrical. "Come to my arms, I beg you," she said in a doleful voice, as if she were still praying. "We have lost our Giovanna," she whispered, hugging me tight. "Now we must pray for her soul."

I broke away from her embrace and looked at her directly. "Giovanna was murdered."

"I know. Inspector Mele was here."

"He suspects me of being the killer."

Prunella caressed my cheek. "You're innocent. I know that."

"Giovanna had a lover."

"I know that too. Carla told me."

"But you don't know who it was?"

"No."

"Giovanna never told you anything about this?"

"She would come here for meals, she would go into her room and shut the door, to rest. She seemed happy to me."

But she wasn't. She had become the slut of the man who had ruined her life. I was tempted to ask Prunella if that phrase had any meaning for her, but I lacked the courage. That woman had been overwhelmed by a tsunami of grief and pain. She was resisting through pure faith.

"We're going to rehearse the hymns for the funeral now," she announced. "Do you want to join us?"

As I left the house I ran into Venerino Stoppa, known as Rino the Embalmer. He invariably carried a black plastic valise with an assortment of coffin catalogues.

"Tomorrow morning, the prosecutor's office is releasing the corpse for the funeral," he announced confidently.

I didn't waste my breath asking him how he knew. Rino always knew things before anyone else. He was a true professional.

Soon I would see Giovanna again. For the last time. A quick visit to the morgue before the coffin was sealed forever. As I got into my car I wondered if I really wanted to see her again.

I had just started the engine when my cell phone rang. I felt a stab at my stomach. Giovanna had selected the ring tone a couple of days before she was murdered. She loved to change my ring tones, and there were times when I lost track so that, among the dozens of cell phones that crowded the court building, I often failed to recognize my own. It was Davide Trevisan.

"First of all, my condolences," he began in dialect.

"Thanks."

"I would have preferred to tell you in person, but I had to call you, because here in the piazza café there's an unpleasant situation that concerns you."

"I don't understand."

"That idiot Filippo has gulped down three Negronis in a row and now he's making a speech. He says that you killed Giovanna and he's going to make you pay for it."

"I'll be right there," I snarled, and snapped the phone shut.

What I should have done was call my father and Inspector Mele. They would have made sure that Filippo shut up and stayed out of sight. But I couldn't take it anymore, and I wanted to pick a fight with someone, anyone. And that psychotic was perfect for it.

I was at the café in three minutes flat. When I walked in the door everyone turned to stare. Half the town was there enjoying the show. Filippo was the only one who failed to notice my presence. He had his back to me. He was arguing with Bepi, the bartender, who was refusing to serve him a fourth Negroni and urging him to go home.

Filippo lost control. "This is a public place of refreshment, and you have a legal obligation to serve me, do you understand?"

"You're drunk, get the hell out of my bar," the barman shot back, shooting a worried glance in my direction.

Filippo pulled a handful of banknotes out of the pocket of his heavy jacket and threw them in Bepi's direction. "I'll buy this stinking bar from you. How much do you want?"

"Bepi's right, you need to go home," I said loudly.

Filippo whipped around and gave me a vicious smile. "Have you come to enjoy your last wine spritzer before going to prison?"

It took three, maybe four steps to cross the bar. I was close enough that if I had reached out my hand, I could have touched him. And that was what I was tempted to do. "Shut your mouth," I ordered him.

Speaking to the other customers, he pointed at me. "He killed Giovanna because she had decided to come back to me."

"Giovanna felt nothing but pity for you. Look at yourself, can't you see what a sad mess you've become?"

Filippo emitted a bloodcurdling scream. It issued from his throat as if I had run him through, and he lunged at me. It was what I wanted, and I was ready for him. I hit him with a left to the jaw and then with a right to the belly. Filippo took the punches better than I expected and hit me in the forehead with an empty glass.

The fight came to a quick end. Strong arms pulled the two of us apart. I couldn't break free, and I quickly found myself outside the café.

"Calm down," said Davide Trevisan as he handed me a handkerchief. The base of the glass had cut my forehead. "I have to say, you're a real half-ass," he mocked me good-naturedly. "You can't even beat up a cripple."

"Fuck you, Davide."

"Come on, you don't need to take it out on me."

"You're right, I'm sorry."

"It's nothing. This is a bad time for you," he said, then he lowered his voice. "And anyway, even if it was you, you're still a friend to me."

I looked at him as if he'd lost his mind. "What are you saying?"

"You can count on me. When they questioned me, I said nothing about the slut who was rubbing your crotch. You know, it takes practically nothing for those guys to get the wrong idea."

I was speechless. I turned and left. Davide was a small-town bar animal. Nothing but dirty jokes and filthy gossip. Now I knew what they thought about me. I almost ran into Beggiolin, who had come running, followed by his cameraman. When he saw me, he had an immediate reaction of fury.

I flashed him a satisfied smile. "You're too late. The party's already over."

* * *

To the women of the town, Antonio Visentin "was still a good-looking man," and according to the men "they don't make them like Antonio Visentin anymore."

This universal opinion was evident every time he crossed the main piazza, which he did four times a day to reach his law office in the center of town.

The men would bow their heads ever so slightly in a sign of intimate respect, or else they would greet him with stage gestures, hoping to ingratiate themselves with those who counted in town.

The women would cast him coquettish glances, or wait anxiously to be recognized and greeted. Which he unfailingly did. Counselor Visentin never missed a trick.

Things went differently that day. As he walked around the piazza under the porticoes, he failed to notice Judge Bellaviti and he avoided the curious glance of the widow Biondi.

Visentin looked at the ground as he walked, lost in dark thoughts. He didn't even notice the uproar outside the Bar Centrale. If he had only looked up, he would have seen his son burst out of the café, arms pinned to his side by Trevisan and other customers.

He had an appointment with the head of the Medical Examiner's Office.

"It's a confidential matter," he had told him over the phone.

Guido Marizza, the head of the Medical Examiner's Office, was an old friend. They had gone to elementary school together, then to middle school and high school.

They'd drifted out of contact during their years at university, because each had followed in his father's footsteps, as had been the case in each family for at least three generations. The sole exception was Marizza's grandfather on his mother's side. He, to the dismay of family and community, had chosen to become a professional soccer player, and wound up playing in the minor minors, the Italian *serie C*. This one unfortunate case aside, no other family member had ever left the beaten track.

Visentin had served as legal counsel to his old friend in a disagreeable case involving an inheritance. He had been successful in the case against Marizza's sisters, relying on the usual nitpicking detail, a formal shortcoming that everyone else had overlooked. Since then, neither of the sisters acknowledged him in public, or spoke to him in private. But his friendship with Guido was as sound as ever. And so he chose to adopt a direct approach. If it hadn't been Guido, he would never have taken such a gross risk. His usual approach could be summed up by the phrase: "Ask for a pear if an apple is what you want." But things were different with Guido.

"I am very worried about Francesco. His alibi lends itself to ambiguous, dangerous interpretations."

Marizza nodded wisely, wrinkling his nose as if he'd noticed a bad smell.

"This matter of the DNA. You know how these things can be, mistakes can be made . . . In other words, Guido, I'd like it if you were personally responsible for doing the testing, and not just one of your assistants. I . . . only trust you."

Marizza gazed at him without expression. "Nowadays, I leave those tests to my assistants, I don't spend much time in the laboratory anymore."

"I would be infinitely grateful," Visentin insisted.

Marizza slumped back into his imposing leather office chair, a gift from his staff for his twenty-year anniversary. He grimaced, as if the stockfish and polenta from the *baccalà alla vicentina* that he'd eaten for lunch had risen to the back of his throat. Then he leaned forward, speaking in an archly confidential tone of voice.

"There's a machine that we use in the forensic lab. About a month ago, it caused a real problem, it skewed the DNA results on a piece of evidence. Luckily, it was just a paternity case, so we were able to rerun the test. But in a case like this . . . If the machine damaged the evidence, it would be impossible to reconstruct. And even if there were still traces of sperm in Giovanna's body, they would no longer be usable. Too much time has gone by."

"I know."

"This involves a murder . . ."

"This involves my Francesco."

"Certainly, certainly."

Visentin realized he'd ventured too far. He shifted tone, as if they had just met at the country club, enjoying a glass of prosecco.

"How is Elisabetta?" he asked.

"She's doing well. She's well liked on the job. They say she's a talented art restorer. I think she's ready to take the next step, but you know what public institutions are like. Talent isn't enough."

"Is Volpi still the director?"

"That stubborn old cuss won't retire . . ."

"Perhaps the time has come to make way for young blood. When this is all over, I could invite the old gentleman to the trout-fishing lake. And let him catch all the trout . . ."

"As long as Elisabetta never finds out. That girl has her mother's sense of pride."

"It'll be our little secret."

The two friends smiled in complicity.

Visentin stood up. "Fine. I'm very pleased."

When he was at the door, Marizza's voice reached him: "Francesco is a good boy, certainly not the kind of boy who would . . ."

"Certainly not," said Visentin, as he turned to look back.

"Fine," Marizza echoed.

There was nothing more to be said.

* * *

Whenever she had an important meeting with Antonio Visentin, the Contessa Selvaggia Calchi Renier made an appointment with her hairdresser. She did it to ensure that her hair gleamed with that coppery highlight that, as Antonio always said, gave her a dangerous resemblance to Rita Hayworth. The irony in all this was that Antonio was the only prominent man in town who had never been her lover. What bound them together was much more important than sex. It was a tie that transcended emotions and had its foundations, one might say, in their shared sense of taste. No one else could claim to have a fraction of the aesthetic sense that Antonio put—not into winning a case, but winning resoundingly, over-winning. No one had a better instinct than he did for the perfect timing in driving home a thrust or withdrawing from an excessively risky business deal without looking weak. Antonio, and Antonio alone, knew how important it was to her to occupy center stage—no matter whether it was a business conference or opening night in a new concert season. If he had never been a lawyer, he could certainly have became a great director: he glimpsed things before others did, he knew how to guide his protagonists, and he knew how to describe—even recount—a new business opportunity to any audience. Antonio had never lorded it over her that he had been born a Visentin, while she had had to become a Contessa. If it hadn't been for Antonio, this difference would have condemned her to a role as a co-star, a decorative gewgaw, a role to which her late husband would gladly have relegated her, if he had been strong enough. She owed the single most important thing to Antonio Visentin: her public recognition. When her husband was still alive, Antonio had encouraged her in her efforts to rejuvenate the ancient fortunes of the Calchi Renier family, he had suggested the best strategies, and he had woven around her that network of consensus that had culminated in the creation of her masterpiece, the Torrefranchi Foundation. It had all happened so quickly, in the few dizzying years in which the Northeast had transformed itself from a land of farmers and emigrants into the wealthiest and most productive industrial region in all of Europe. A free-market network, a promised land of productivity that not even the most reactionary and pompous apparatus of government intervention could hobble or restrict. This is what she and Antonio had in common: a love of the modern, a love of the new.

Now times were changing again, and even faster this go-round. That was why she was worried. She needed Antonio more than ever, his strength and his courage. Giovanna's death and the suspicions hovering over Francesco threatened to ruin everything. Now it was up to her to build, to fabricate if necessary, a public acknowledgment toward the Visentin family. A public acknowledgment of innocence.

"Contessa, we are home," announced the Romanian chauffeur as he parked the black Mercedes in front of the staircase of Villa Selvaggia.

"Thank you, Toader, I won't be needing the car again today."

As she climbed the steps with a gait that a thirty-year-old woman would have envied, Giorgio, the imperishable butler of the Calchi Renier family, stepped forward and announced: "Counselor Visentin is waiting for you, Madame Contessa."

"Ask the cook to prepare a karkade tea." She wasted no mawkish sentiment on Giorgio; he was a reminder of her husband, and just as much of a snob as he had been while he lived. If it weren't for Filippo's objections, she would have sent him to a nursing home long since.

"Immediately, Contessa," said the butler with a ceremonious bow.

"Contessa," Selvaggia thought to herself. This title of respect, with which she was addressed by housemaids, butlers, chauffeurs, superintendents, secretaries, lawyers, business partners, executives, union leaders, prelates, and accountants, still stirred her soul. Contessa is a title usually acquired at birth. She had become a Contessa, eradicating completely her station at birth, eliminating even her peasant surname.

As she swept into her office, Antonio rose promptly to greet her with that unfailing gallantry that he would display even if there were a cocked pistol held to his forehead. But his expression was glum, and Selvaggia immediately had her worst fears confirmed.

"I have just been informed that our sons have exchanged blows at the Bar Centrale. I'll spare you the details," said Visentin.

The Contessa rolled her eyes heavenward. "That's not helpful." She patted the empty space on the sofa by her side. "Sit here, next to me," she said with a kindness she never used with anyone else, not even with Filippo.

Visentin heaved a sigh. He pulled a cigar out of his inside jacket packet. "Do you mind if I smoke?"

She smiled. "You know I like the smell of your cigars."

Antonio lit his cigar a little more hastily than usual. He leaned back into the backrest of the late Venetian sofa.

"You must persuade Filippo to withdraw his statement," he said and, after gazing into her eyes thoughtfully for a long moment, he added: "And if Filippo were by chance to remember that he left Francesco a little later in the morning, Francesco would be entirely free of suspicion."

"Filippo will do precisely what I tell him, rest assured," the Contessa shot back confidently. "However, considering the way matters now stand, the new version of his testimony will not be enough. Idle gossip can be more damaging than an appeal-proof verdict, as you long ago taught me. We must think of the Foundation. The business structure is in a very delicate phase of transition, as you know all too well."

"What do you have in mind?"

Selvaggia saw a gleam in the eyes of her personal lawyer. She smiled at that virtually imperceptible manifestation of vitality. "We need a public acknowledgment."

She intentionally used those precise words, even if Antonio at that juncture would be unable to grasp their more profound meaning. "We own a broadcasting company. Let's use it." And in order to leave Visentin the time necessary to appreciate her strategy, she plucked the cigar from his fingers and indulged in a deep and voluptuous drag.

"Well, maybe that reporter at Antenna N/E, Beggiolin. He has a big following in town."

"That's exactly who I was thinking of," smiled Selvaggia, returning his cigar to him.

* * *

My father lived in an Art Nouveau villa that had belonged to one of the earliest major industrialists in the area—a pioneer in the field of farm machinery. His factory was demolished decades ago, and his heirs had chosen to change their line of work and place of residence. My father bought the villa immediately after my mother's death and I had never lived in it, what with boarding school and the university. Papa decided not to remarry, and his only companions were his domestic servants and the family of the concierge who had lived with him for many years now.

Severina, the concierge's wife, opened the gate for me and gave me a melancholy smile. Sergio, the butler, opened the door just as my finger was about to touch the buzzer. He greeted me with a deferential hauteur, like a movie butler, and showed me into the living room. A comforting fire was crackling in the little fireplace. Papa sat watching television. He gestured for me to sit down beside him.

On the screen I saw the images of the piazza and the café. Beggiolin appeared on screen, pointing to the interior of the café.

"Here, in the Bar Centrale, a few minutes ago, according to reports from numerous eyewitnesses, Filippo Calchi Renier and Francesco Visentin engaged in a fistfight. That alone would be a minor piece of news—though we must say that when two scions of two such important and respected families brawl in public, the town's image is badly tarnished as a result—were it not for one significant detail. Filippo Calchi

Renier has publicly accused Francesco Visentin of murdering his own fiancée, the unfortunate Giovanna Barovier . . ."

My father picked up the remote control and turned the television off.

"Nice work," he said with a cutting tone. "They've been running and rerunning this piece for more than an hour. They stop for a commercial break, and then they run it again."

"I know, I made a mistake. I'm sorry."

"You have no excuses, Francesco. And don't try to feed me nonsense about being upset and losing control. There are things you just don't do. It could result in my being hauled before the board of the order, and as you know, I'm the chairman. I would have no choice but to resign."

He stood up and went to pour himself a glass of prosecco from a bottle chilling in an elegant silver ice bucket. "In any case, that's not the main problem. You displayed yourself to the world as a violent individual incapable of self-control," he went on. "And everyone will feel justified in assuming that you killed Giovanna."

"To tell the truth, that's what they already think."

He ignored my comment. "From this moment on, you will do nothing on your own initiative. You will do only what I tell you to do. I will take care of everything. I've already arranged to take care of the evidence, and tomorrow evening we will go and have a talk with Filippo."

"What evidence are you talking about?"

"The sperm. I talked to Marizza, we won't have any surprises."

I stood up and grabbed the wineglass out of his hand. "Why did you do that? Do you think I'm guilty?"

"No. But you can never be too sure in cases like this one. I've been a lawyer for too many years to leave things to chance. One mistake and you're screwed. It would be just one more piece of evidence against you because, in case you haven't grasped the point, you have no alibi after two in the morning, and Giovanna was killed between one and three."

"The DNA test of the sperm doesn't prove anything. I could easily have killed her after her lover left the house."

"Precisely. Which is why it is advisable to get rid of any elements that could make your position any worse."

I smashed the glass on the floor. "Instead of worrying about me, an innocent man, you should pressure Zan to find the man who killed her. All you need to do is pick up the telephone, and that incompetent fool would actually be forced to do some genuine investigating."

My father pointed to the shattered glass on the wet floor. "You see?" he said, in an exaggeratedly calm tone of voice. "You are incapable of dealing with the situation."

"I want to know why you don't pick up that fucking phone."

"Moderate your language," he warned me. "There's a time for everything. First and foremost, I want to be absolutely sure that you aren't implicated. Then we'll think about the investigation. Giovanna was like a daughter to me. You know how much I loved her."

"This is only helping the murderer to get away with it."

He shrugged. "I can't help it if Zan is incompetent," he said in an irritated tone of voice. "And he can't pursue multiple lines of investigation at the same time. Breathing down his neck would do no good at all. We must make the right moves at the right time."

"Then why not have him replaced?"

He shook his head in disappointment at my naïveté. "That would be the worst possible move. Everyone would think that I had taken him off the case because he had you dead to rights."

* * *

Adalberto Beggiolin was known in the circles he frequented by the nickname of "puddle shark," a cold-blooded predator that foraged in shallow, filthy waters.

He was hardly a sniper with a high-precision rifle. He was more comfortable working with a sawed-off shotgun. If you shoot into the crowd, you're sure to hit something. He looked on newsgathering as an activity akin to carpet bombing. In his view, good reporting resulted in bleeding, screaming victims.

He was therefore somewhat disconcerted when, following Giovanna Barovier's death, he received no specific instructions on who to target, either from the station owner or his own producer. Left to his own devices, a predator of his caliber turned blind and stupid. His instinct had led him to savage the first red meat that bumped up against his snout, but this time he'd mistaken his prey.

His reports on Francesco Visentin and Filippo Calchi Renier had increased the station's ratings, but something told him that this time he'd fired into the wrong knot of bystanders.

What Beggiolin lacked was prudence, discernment, and the gift of self-censorship. That was why he failed to make it up to the level of the national broadcast news; that was why he was still swimming in circles in the puddle of local society news; he had become a big fish in a small pond.

When he was summoned for a meeting with the Contessa, he prepared himself for the worst; he knew that this time he had pissed on the Persian carpet.

He gulped down the last bit of meatball sandwich that he'd packed for lunch that morning, and left the newsroom without a word to anyone.

On his way over to the Villa Selvaggia, he tried to remember everything he knew about the Contessa.

He remembered the things that everyone knew, including the fact that through the Foundation she controlled 70 percent of Antenna N/E.

In particular, though, he recalled her exaggeratedly protective instinct toward her slightly deranged son.

He had seen them together, about a year earlier, in the local prison.

The Torrefranchi Foundation had announced a program for the reintegration into society and rehabilitation of convicts released from prison. The slogan was: "Let's give them another chance." The Contessa had been impeccable in her introductory speech. She had dominated that audience of criminals and convicts with a style worthy of a sadomaso dominatrix. Then she had given the floor to her son, who had spent fifteen embarrassing minutes struggling to deliver a short speech that he had committed to memory along with a fistful of sedatives. It was like watching a pathetic Christmas ritual, with Filippo playing the part of the timid and intimidated child reciting a saccharine little poem, continuously seeking his mother's approval, as she fed him word after word, her lips moving in silent unison.

That woman was a remarkable piece of work: one minute she was Margaret Thatcher addressing the House of Lords, a minute later she was a worried mother, looking down at her badly brought-up son with a look of beautiful concern.

As Beggiolin made his way through the spacious drawing rooms of the Villa Selvaggia, he had no illusions. He was expecting the tigress to greet him by clamping her fangs down hard, not certainly by licking the back of his hand.

He obediently trailed along behind the butler, doing his best not to let the bloody scenes of hunting depicted on the villa's walls unnerve him excessively. His legs were beginning to shake. He hoped he wouldn't have to remain standing during the interview.

Luckily, it only lasted five minutes. And it turned out fine. Firing a shotgun blast into the crowd; that was his specialty. That was basically what the Contessa had said to him. Of

course, she hadn't used those exact words. What she had really said was: "The important thing is to take a clear stand.
Unsettling things are happening in town. Elderly women have
been attacked in their homes over the past few months, and
the police are no closer to catching the culprit than they were
before. Why don't you talk about that? Perhaps poor Giovanna ran afoul of these same cowards. It's only a hypothesis,
of course. Other ideas can be developed. I don't want to tell
you how to do your job. I leave the details to you. One last
thing: the young Francesco Visentin will soon be cleared of
suspicion, and it strikes me that, when the time is right, he
deserves to have his reputation fully and amply rehabilitated,
don't you agree?"

He sure did think so. The Contessa had given him the
scent, and he had charged off like a pack of bloodhounds in
full bay. The following morning he was in the office early, and
he worked until the middle of the afternoon to put together a
blue-ribbon report announced by teasers throughout the
broadcast day.

It was 8 P.M., and the prime-time television news was coming on. His piece was the opening report, and in the town tavern, the Osteria Dalla Mora, the fans were cheering as if at a
championship soccer game.

For Beggiolin, it was like attending the premiere of a film
he had directed.

As the special report on the home invasion gang was being
broadcast, he watched the audience react in unison just as orig-
inally intended. Their anger was being goaded to a fury, chan-
neled in precisely the direction desired by the Contessa. "Out-
siders," "people that aren't from around here," blacks, Alba-
nians, and Moroccans. They were obviously the guilty parties,
they were the ones that the police and the Carabinieri simply
refused to go after.

Beggiolin knew his audience, and he knew it well. Small

businessmen who had become arrogant with the rivers of cash they had made in the eighties and nineties, and who were now wetting their pants at the prospect of being swept away by their hungry and ambitious Chinese rivals. It's always these fucking Chinese. First they were Communists, now they're capitalists, and all the while the factories are laying off workers, closing down, moving out of the region or out of the country. Craftsmen, businessmen, restaurateurs with increasingly empty wallets. A vast populace that hadn't appreciated their good luck while they had it, who had felt invincible before—but who now felt only fear. Fear and anger. And the anger was growing rapidly because they couldn't blame the usual crowd of thieves running the government, now that the government was being run by people just like them—irate businessmen and media tycoons. And so they turned to the television, hoping to hear something other than the usual reports from the front.

But that evening, the television, in the person of Adalberto Beggiolin, had suggested to them a very simple little idea, not at all complicated, easy to grasp. It was all the fault of the barbarian invasions. Negroes who had come to town to steal our jobs, Moroccans who were selling drugs to school kids, black women selling sex for a few dollars on every street corner, diabolical temptresses who were stealing good husbands from the family hearth. Young Serbian and Hungarian women who didn't know how to clean house or cook meals, but who were eminently capable of taking local boys to bed and conniving them into proposing marriage.

In the news report, the women were angriest. There was no upside to prostitution for them, while their husbands on the other hand had a certain vested interest to protect.

As he leaned against the counter in the tavern, Beggiolin caressed his audience with his gaze. Some of them he knew personally. Aldo Trolese, a former employee of the electric company ENEL, now retired and working as a cabinet maker, a good old boy unless he got started on his third bottle of red. Tommaso Nadal, a human refrigerator and the owner of a moving company. Tommaso always wore two leather wrist-bands, even when he went to sleep at night. They made him look like one of those bewhiskered warriors who fought against or alongside Conan the Barbarian.

Then there was Elide Squizzato. Actually, she was present in two forms, physically in the tavern but also in the video. Beggiolin had chosen to interview her because of her incredible facility for weeping on cue. All you had to do was get her to say the word "negro" and she turned red as a beet and teared up as if someone had let off a tear-gas grenade under her nose. During the course of the man-in-the-street interview with her that Beggiolin had done "by chance," he had cajoled her into pronouncing the magic word on three separate occasions, and poor Elide had failed to complete her thought after the third, her shoulders shuddering in sobs. All the same, the idea came across quite clearly: whatever it was the blacks had done to her, it certainly must have been something horrible.

As the special report on Antenna N/E was about to make its triumphant début, three young men entered the café. They looked like club-goers with a homicidal edge. They had gotten out of a Jeep Cherokee; Beggiolin had noticed them outside the tavern window.

They burst into the place whooping like wild Indians, and showing off for their supposed audience.

Instead of obtaining the desired effect, and that is, frightening the clientele for pure fun, they were rudely hushed by Maso, that is Tommaso Nadal, the moving man.

"Why, what's on, a soccer game?" the skinniest of the three asked in some wonderment. He was the only one of the group that Beggiolin thought he recognized. His name was Denis, and his father was an insurance salesman.

"Ah, shut up and sit down," somebody yelled from the back of the tavern.

The three of them considered the situation. The tavern was packed, but there were little old ladies, and lots of pants-wetters, like that guy over there, that loudmouth from the TV, leaning on the bar.

If they wanted to, they could have really caused some mayhem.

Rocco was already grabbing a chair while the audience was shouting more loudly for quiet, but Lucio stopped him, putting one hand on his wrist and jutting his chin at the television.

Rocco turned to look at the TV, and Denis did the same thing, in sheep-like emulation.

On the big screen, Elide had just managed to stop sobbing, and she had been replaced by an old woman in a pink dressing gown standing in front of a hospital bed. She was pointing a knobby, trembling finger at an imaginary attacker (Lucio felt as if she were pointing directly at him), cursing him and calling down the agonies of the inferno upon him, because: "It's not right to do things like that to a poor old woman, you shouldn't beat a defenseless grandmother, you shouldn't steal her life savings—she's just a poor woman with no one to protect her." In conclusion, with a surprising upwelling of strength, displaying her yellowed teeth and faceful of wrinkles, she hissed repeatedly, an uncounted number of times: "Criminals."

She was unquestionably having a certain effect on her audience.

Lucio looked around. The customers of the tavern had leapt to their feet, and several were clapping the television guy on his shoulder as he stood leaning against the bar.

Everyone was shouting so loud that no one could understand a word.

Rocco was mystified, and so was Denis.

But Lucio was the boss. And he had understood perfectly.

He started shouting loudest of all: "Let's give 'em a lesson, these black bastards!"

It had the desired effect. With a single harsh command, he had managed to channel that rancorous muttering, that sterile frenzy into a brutal, ferocious, and even joyful explosion of fury.

Lucio and Beggiolin's eyes locked in a rapid flash, and it was as if they had recognized one another.

Then the wave washed away from Beggiolin, surging toward the three young men who had arrived in the Cherokee; they threw open the door and left the tavern, followed by all the men under sixty-five years of age.

The hunt was officially on.

Babacar Ngoup was about to make a momentous decision. He was fed up with trying to sell carved hardwood elephants and bootleg CDs; eighty percent of the take went to the district manager; what was left over was barely enough for room and board. He could barely spare anything for remittances, and back home, his little sister was about to get married.

Babacar was a tall, skinny, young man, with a small shapely nose that drove the women crazy, especially certain Italian women.

He had never studied. It wasn't because he had lacked the opportunity, though. It was because he didn't feel like it. Like all the young people he'd grown up with in Senegal, he wanted to make music, he wanted to become a star like Youssou N'Dour and sing duets with a babe like Neneh Cherry. He was sick and fucking tired of humping that duffel bag back and forth all day in the fog that chilled your bones. The fog weighed him down with a melancholy that took away any desire to sing. He had what it took to be a star, but what he lacked was everything else. Lately, he didn't even have a girlfriend, and that had never happened before—not even in Italy. He came from a family of *tombeurs de femmes*, lady-killers. His father had had five wives. His grandfather had had fifteen, plus lots of others. His grandfather was a griot, a storyteller. He had a way with words. He told beautiful stories—ghost stories and love stories—and he knew how to enchant anyone, especially the women. The women gobbled him up with their eyes from the front doors of their houses.

Babacar had the gift of words too, but what good was that in a town where hardly anyone even spoke French? *Merde!* It was eight in the evening, and there wasn't a living soul in sight. Back in Dakar, life was just beginning at that time of night.

Je me suis emmerdé, he thought. He was really sick and tired.

So he'd made up his mind: That night, he would tuck twenty grams of cocaine into his duffel bag. He'd sell the coke, use the money to produce his first CD, and buy a ticket to Paris.

That noise made him uneasy. What was it? A pack of ghosts, that's how his grandfather would have described it. He'd lived in that town for two years, and every night for the past two years he'd waited at the same bus stop for his ride home. He'd never heard anything like this. Voices, footsteps, and a roaring undertone, like feedback from an electric bass. Whatever it was, the best thing to do was to *aller vite*. He'd never had problems before, but *il y a toujours une première fois*.

He picked up the duffel bag, which just then weighed him down as if it were as heavy as a boulder.

He took a step backward, peering into the fog.

He felt the beams of automobile headlights on his face; these beams were unusually high. The bright lights immediately made him feel vaguely guilty. On either side of the car, blurry shadows were moving toward him, like so many zombies. They did not seem to be walking on the ground.

Babacar stumbled and fell backward, landing on the edge

of the sidewalk in a seated position. He could feel the wet pavement through the cloth of his trousers. He immediately tried to get up, but something hard hit him on the ear. He fell back to the ground, stunned. The zombies shouted something he couldn't understand. The doors of the tall automobile swung open, and two more shadows got out.

"*Arretez*," he yelled, but the pack had caught his scent, the scent of blood.

He saw one of the shadows that had stepped out of the vehicle raise a weirdly long arm.

He heard the shadow say: "Ciao, brother."

Then the long arm swung down at him, striking him between his neck and his shoulder.

He hurled himself onto his duffel bag. He desperately clawed at the outer pocket in search of his knife, only to feel his knuckles crunch under the heel of a cowboy boot. A sharp kick to the base of his spine throttled the scream in his throat. He understood that this was only the beginning. Kicks, clubs, and chains rained down on his ribs and kidneys. A crowbar shattered one of his legs, a sharp kick to the face broke the bridge of his nose.

He lost consciousness.

Then someone poured some water on him. He thought to himself they must be trying to wake him back up so he could feel more pain. But it wasn't water. His jacket reeked of gasoline. As one of his grandfather's songs pointed out: "With a bit of good luck, there's always a can of gas in someone's truck." He screamed, and it sounded to his ears like the cry of a lobster being dropped into boiling water. It must have startled someone, because instead of burning him, they set fire to his duffel bag.

Or maybe it was the siren of the arriving police car that sent them scattering.

Curled up on the ground, he heard the roar of the turbo

diesel engine as the car disappeared into the distance and running footsteps moving away in all directions.

He managed to open one eye—he could only open the one—and he saw an absurd little man, wearing an enormous heavy jacket and with the rumpled hair of a madman, dancing gleefully around the flaming duffel bag. He seemed like a chimpanzee terrified by fire.

When the Carabiniere squad car pulled up beside the bus stop, the fog was tinged the bluish color of the car's emergency lights. Just before he passed out again, Babacar saw the chimpanzee vanish, in a series of outlandish leaps, under the porticoes.

The chimpanzee was the village fool. No one even remembered his name. Everyone called him "El Mato"—the lunatic. He survived through the charity of parishioners. As long as anyone could remember, he'd worn an old green parka, and no one knew exactly where he lived. He never bothered anyone. From time to time he'd shout out disconnected phrases, but everyone ignored him.

El Mato, prancing along under the porticoes, ran into a man who was pushing an old bicycle beside him. Hanging from the handlebars was a plastic shopping bag, from which protruded the neck of a large wine bottle. El Mato eyed the man curiously. The man wore his long grey hair gathered into a ponytail at the nape of his neck.

"It's you. I recognize you. Now I understand! Now I've figured it out!" he started yelling, pointing the man out to an imaginary crowd.

The man looked around. He thought of hitting the little man to make him shut up, but getting drawn into a brawl was too risky. He got on his bicycle and pedaled quickly away, looking back as he went to make sure that no one was looking out a window. Then he was gone.

Behind him, the madman continued shouting, "Now I understand! Now I've figured it out!"

Hunched over the handlebars, the man knew instantly that that obsessive mantra would keep from him sleeping for the rest of the night.

* * *

My father came to get me immediately after dinner. A sharp honk of the car horn told me he had arrived. During the trip we rode in silence. It was only after he turned the key, stilling the Jaguar's engine, that he warned me to keep my cool, whatever the cost.

The butler led us into the Contessa's study. Selvaggia was intent on a game of two-handed pinochle with Filippo. She stood up, greeted my father with a kiss, and then gave me a chilly hug, producing a series of formal phrases. Filippo kept his back turned to us, and only turned around to face us when scolded by his mother.

He looked at me with scorn. "So now we're inviting murderers to dinner, too?"

I turned toward Papa. "I told you this would be a waste of time."

"I am not interested in the petty quarrels of you two spoiled brats," the Contessa said in a calm, almost bored tone of voice. "You both wound up on the television news for a disgusting brawl, and the time has come to settle things."

"I hope they give you a life sentence, without parole," Filippo hissed.

Selvaggia lost her patience. "That night you weren't at home. If you insist, I'll go personally to see the prosecutor and tell him you're lying. And if you weren't with Francesco, exactly where were you at that time of night?"

"Filippo, please try to reason," my father broke in with a harsh tone of voice. "Each of you represents the other's alibi. You could come under suspicion yourself, everyone knows about your disappointment over Giovanna. You might have felt resentment after the car crash . . ."

Selvaggia grabbed Filippo by the shoulders. "Giovanna was murdered while you two boys were together, and if you make an effort, you will surely remember that you parted company after 3 A.M."

Filippo hung his head, in a mute gesture of capitulation. His mother stroked his head.

"All settled, then," my father said with satisfaction. "Tomorrow morning we'll go to see Zan and you'll correct all your earlier statements."

Filippo looked at me with contempt. "I told you that Giovanna would betray you too."

"Shut your mouth," I said flatly.

"There's no question about the matter," the Contessa broke in. "You have to admit and deal with it, Francesco."

"Please, Selvaggia," my father grumbled.

"I'm telling him for his own good," the Contessa continued. "Francesco will have to face the town. The inconsolable cuckold is a role for losers."

I turned on my heel and left without saying goodbye. My father caught up with me a few minutes later.

"You know what Selvaggia's like," he said, justifying her, as he got in the car. "She never liked Giovanna."

I didn't answer. That woman was a snake, but my mind was occupied by very different thoughts.

"It could have been him," I suddenly said.

"Him who?"

"Filippo."

"Don't talk nonsense."

"Just like me, he has no alibi. Giovanna would have let him into her house even at that time of night, and most important—he had a motive."

"Oh, come on, can you imagine Filippo killing someone?"

I thought about it for a few seconds. "Yes," I answered with conviction.

Papa sighed. "You're not planning to talk about this to Zan or Mele, are you?"

"Why shouldn't I?"

"Because, tomorrow Filippo is going to supply an alibi for both of you. You were together until after three in the morning."

"But what if it really was him who killed her?"

Papa huffed impatiently. "Well, there needs to be other evidence to prove that."

We rode in silence until the Jaguar pulled up outside my front door. As I reached out to open the car door, I was suddenly struck by a thought. "And if that evidence emerged, and if Filippo wound up in jail, Selvaggia would ask you to defend him, wouldn't she?"

"Probably."

"And would you take the case?"

"I don't know. I doubt it. There would probably be a conflict of interest. Giovanna was a lawyer in my law firm . . ."

"She was also my fiancée," I pointed out, angrily.

"Certainly, your fiancée," he hastily agreed. "But now stop obsessing about these fanciful ideas and let the detectives do their work."

Papa pushed his foot down on the acclerator and the Jaguar slid away into the night. My father was wrong. Tomorrow, Filippo would cease to be a suspect for the investigators, once and for all. The more I thought about it, the more reasonable it seemed that he might be the killer. Now that I was out of the picture, Mele and Zan would wonder about him, too. But they wouldn't waste time investigating him as a lead. Filippo had an alibi now. And I had provided that alibi.

I slipped the keys back into my pocket and started walking. I needed to clear my head, think logically about Filippo. By the time I walked out onto the piazza, I was ready to rule him out as the killer. Giovanna had said that she had become the slut of the man who had ruined her life. And that couldn't be Filippo. If anything, it was the other way around. And she would never have made love with him. I knew that deep down. The man who killed her had also been her secret lover. He had killed her because Giovanna had decided to confess everything to me. And he had chosen to drown her rather than let that happen.

The next morning I hung a sign on the front door of my law office: "Closed for Mourning." My father took care of all my scheduled hearings in court; he unleashed all his young lawyers and paralegals to fill in for me. As I walked down the street, I withstood the inquiring gazes with nonchalance. Even though I knew I was innocent, I was still relieved to feel certain that Filippo's new statement would eliminate me as a suspect. I walked over to the Visentin law office. After exchanging a few polite phrases of condolence with the secretaries, I finally managed to get into Giovanna's office and close the door behind me. I sat down at her desk, and I observed my own smiling face—in an elegant frame next to the computer—and I wondered where I should begin my search. There must have been some traces of her relationship with her lover. A note scribbled in her desk diary, an email, a private note. And the telephone, of course. But the investigators would take care of examining the phone records. I began by rummaging through the desk drawers. Nothing there. Then I started the computer, and looked through her email messages—luckily, they weren't password-protected. There was only business correspondence. I was on the wrong trail. There was a knock at the door. It was Inspector Mele. He sat down across from me, in a blue-grey office chair. The chair was a tad too modern for the austere style of the law offices.

"Find anything?" he asked with a smile.

I shook my head.

"I've already gone over it with a fine-toothed comb," he told me. "But I certainly could have missed something."

He set his police hat down on the table. With slow and carefully calibrated movements, he turned the hat around and tucked his black leather gloves into it. Then he unzipped his police jacket. "This morning, Filippo Calchi Renier, accompanied by your father, went to see Zan," he said in a neutral tone of voice. "He retracted his earlier testimony, and now he has removed all suspicion from you. Luckily, he has fully recovered his memory, and, in the end, he was even more precise than you were. While Giovanna was being killed, the two of you were reminiscing about the good old days."

The sarcasm, too, was carefully calibrated.

"You don't seem very convinced."

"It's obvious that you two came to an understanding after your little brawl in the café, but that doesn't interest me. It wasn't either of you. Of that I am quite sure."

"What about Zan?"

"He's happy to have you out from underfoot. He's afraid of your father, as you well know."

"And you?"

He shrugged. "The worst they could do is transfer me. If I'm lucky, they'll send me back to southern Italy, where I'm from."

The inspector sat in silence, staring at me. I felt uncomfortable.

"She was murdered by her lover," I blurted out after a couple of minutes.

He nodded in agreement. "Probably, but the only male fingerprints in Giovanna's house were yours. Doesn't that strike you as odd?"

"He must have wiped them off . . ."

"Without wiping away the others?" he asked, doubtfully.

He had a point. That made no sense. "What about her diary, and the phone records?"

"I shouldn't tell you this, because the investigation is still in progress. But we haven't found anything solid."

"That can't be. Giovanna and her lover must have communicated somehow."

He spread his arms in resignation. "I can't figure it out. And in any case, I have to obey Zan's order, I have no freedom of initiative." He picked up his hat and gloves and got to his feet. "Well, now you know how matters stand," he said, heading toward the door.

"How did you know I was here?"

"I had you followed," he answered flatly. "But after Filippo Calchi Renier's new statement, the order was revoked. I'll see you tomorrow at the funeral."

"The killer will be there too," I ventured in a small voice.

"The whole town will be there," Mele shot back.

A little later, my father arrived as well. "Everything's taken care of," he said. "You're no longer under investigation."

"Now it's up to you, Papa. You have to make that phone call. Zan has to begin investigating for real."

"Don't worry about that. I'll get busy, today." Then he looked around the room. "It seems impossible—to walk into this room and not find Giovanna," he said sadly.

"She told Carla Pisani that she wanted to confess everything to me, because she had become the slut of the man who had ruined her life. Who do you think she could have been talking about?"

Papa sat down on the same office chair where the inspector had been sitting just a few minutes earlier. He ran his fingers through his hair. "I couldn't say. When I read your friend's statement I was very surprised. Maybe that's Pisani's interpretation of the facts. You know how witnesses can react under pressure."

"No," I answered decisively. "Carla repeated Giovanna's exact words. I'm sure of it."

"Then I can't understand how this lover could have ruined her life. The whole episode with Alvise goes back fifteen years. Ever since then, Giovanna had put her life back together, with hard work. She had a degree in law and a promising professional future—"

"And tomorrow she was going to become my wife."

"Exactly, as you can see that statement just doesn't make sense. Now, if you'll excuse me, I have an appointment with a client."

I sat there a while longer, lost in thought. Then I took my photograph off the desk and tossed it into the trash.

Beggiolin reported on Filippo's change in testimony during the lunch hour news show. Oddly, he used a very sober tone in his reporting. Then he aired a sidebar about me. I saw myself in my lawyer's robes, in court, delivering a summation. Beggiolin must have considered me innocent, because he used unfailingly positive language. The message to the town was unmistakable and would be duly accepted. After announcing the funeral, scheduled for the following morning at ten, in the church of San Prosdocimo, however, the television reporter engaged in a little extra dollop of muckraking. Quoting an unnamed but highly reliable source, he talked about the semen found in Giovanna's body. He made no further comment, but he did stare for a few extra beats into the lens, with a cynical smile impressed on his lips.

I got rid of him by punching a button on my remote control, and then I moved into the kitchen. I wasn't hungry, and my stomach was queasy with tension. I peered into the fridge and rummaged through the pantry. I decided to make a plate of pasta with butter. Whenever I was sick, that was the dish my mother would make for me. A pat of butter, a little milk, and grated parmesan cheese. I had decided not to leave the house until the funeral. After lunch, I'd take a couple of Giovanna's sleeping pills. I wanted to knock myself out and just stop thinking. Instead, as soon as I had drained the pot of bowties, Carla rang the buzzer.

"Have you already eaten?" I asked her at the door.

Her only reply was to try to punch me in the face. I grabbed her wrist. "Whoa, take it easy. What's that for?"

Carla was panting with rage. "So you made a little arrangement after all, didn't you? First you accuse each other, then you swap alibis."

"Get out of here, you don't know what you're talking about," I snarled at her. I tried to shut the door, but she wouldn't let me.

"I should have known this is how it would end up. The Visentins and the Calchi Reniers can't afford a scandal. So that's how you arrange things. Tomorrow, they're going to bury Giovanna, and the truth will go down into the grave with her body. This town will never change. And you're no better than the rest of them."

I seized her by the shoulders and started to shake her. Her purse dropped to the floor, and she stared at me in fright. I let her go. She bent down to pick up her purse, and then turned and fled down the stairs.

"Don't you ever dare speak to me like that again," I shouted after her.

I tossed the pasta into the garbage. I was furious. I wanted to run out the door after her, I wanted to shout into her surprised face that, more than anything else, what I wanted to see was Giovanna's murderer in handcuffs, flanked by a pair of Carabinieri. It was as those thoughts ran through my mind that a light shone into my mind. I suddenly glimpsed the price I would have to pay to ensure that the murderer went to prison. At the trial, the killer would tell the court all about his relationship with Giovanna. The lawyers and the prosecutor would want to probe for further details. How had they first met? How many dates? How often did they make love behind my back? The killer would swear that he loved her and never wanted to hurt her. In the eyes of the court, Giovanna would be remembered as his woman. I would fade into the background. The pathetic figure of the cuckolded fiancé, demanding justice. As a lawyer, I immediately reckoned up the likely sentence. Sixteen years, give or take a few. That was the price set on Giovanna's life. I forced myself to take a hard look at my consience. Was I really willing to pay that price for revenge?

I seized a bottle at random from the tray and poured myself a glassful of liquor. I gulped it down with the sleeping pills.

Pale rays of sunlight illuminated one of the coldest mornings of the year. My father, Prunella, and I followed the hearse as it left the morgue.

"This was supposed to be the happiest day of my life," Prunella said suddenly, breaking into a doleful silence.

Right. This was supposed to have been a day of celebration. I would have stood waiting for her by the altar, and she would appear at the head of the aisle on my father's arm. She would walk slowly down the aisle, smiling and nodding her head at various guests. I slipped a hand into my pocket, and my fingers touched the case containing the two wedding rings. I had decided to have them buried with her body.

Inspector Mele was right. Giovanna's funeral was a spectacle that no one in town would miss for any reason. Those who had been unable to find a place to sit in the church itself crowded the church courtyard and a substantial portion of the main piazza. The citizenry watched our arrival in silence. Many made the sign of the cross when they saw us. When we stepped out of our car, we were approached by our closest acquaintances and by the leading citizens of the town. Selvaggia, elegant in her black overcoat with a fur collar, hurried to embrace Prunella. Filippo stood off to one side, in isolation.

"My poor Prunella," she exclaimed loudly. "Misfortune seems to follow you everywhere. But you're always so strong."

Her voice and her face were intently acting out the role of a bereaved Contessa, but her eyes told an entirely different story. Selvaggia never missed a chance to settle old scores. Prunella noticed it, and reddened with fury, but she was quickly surrounded by her prayer group, which immediately struck up a hymn to the Lord, and accompanied her into the church. I followed close behind the coffin, resting one hand on the dark polished wood. I wanted to be sure that everyone saw that the cuckold had decided to follow his destiny to its logical conclusion. Carla was already seated in the front row. She made a big show of ignoring me. Don Piero and Don Ante stood waiting by the altar. The old priest conducted the ceremony. He recalled Giovanna with a short but affectionate speech. He concluded by warning the murderer that he would face the Lord's wrath. Prunella and her friends distinguished themselves with a series of prayers recited with a level of fervor that struck me as unsettling. Their arms flung outward in imitation of Jesus Christ on the cross, and their faces turned heavenward clearly irritated Don Piero as well; from time to time he glared angrily over at the group.

When the coffin was carried out of the church, my hand was still there, resting on the gleaming cherry wood. Beggiolin pointed me out to the cameraman, who took a long steady shot. It was at that very moment that Inspector Mele came over and shook my hand firmly. Mele had also decided to transmit a precise signal.

Beggiolin raised the microphone to his lips. "The whole town has turned out to pay tribute to Giovanna Barovier; it is certainly not mere rhetoric to speak of a young life shattered in the bloom of youth, just a few steps short of the crowning dream of love with her own Francesco."

Beggiolin was capable of staining anything with just his tone of voice. I wanted to pound his face with both fists, but this was neither the place nor the time for that.

When the coffin was loaded onto the hearse, as if by magic El Mato appeared, kneeling and crying out: "Now I understand! Now I've figured it out!"

Mele gently seized him by the scruff of the neck and handed him over him to a pair of young Carabinieri.

Half an hour later it was all over. I walked away from the cemetery with an image in my head of the gravedigger who had sealed the tomb with cement strolling away, lighting a cigarette as he went.

I had been slumped on the sofa for hours. My mind was buzzing with images from the funeral. Faces familiar and unknown. Among them was the murderer—of that I felt certain. Perhaps he had even shaken my hand and expressed his sincere condolences. But I hadn't singled out any prime suspect. The killer would have to be charming, elegant, young, and a member of the upper crust. I knew Giovanna well. She had strong opinions when it came to men and the social circles in which they moved. Mele probably didn't know quite what to look for. Lovers communicate in secret codes. If they were bold enough to meet at Giovanna's house, they must have had some way of being certain I wouldn't walk in on them. I ransacked my memory for the perfect times to meet behind my back. On Tuesdays I played volleyball on the covered field at the country club, and then, after the usual quick stop by the wine bar, I went straight to bed. But I always called her before falling asleep to say goodnight. How many times had she whispered sweet nothings over the phone to me while he lay at her side, breathing, waiting? I pictured her to myself, her hair damp and matted after a bout of lovemaking. Tuesdays might very well have been their standing date. Then, there were times that I had to work late in my law office, preparing a case. On those evenings, perhaps, she alerted him.

"Francesco has to work tonight. I'll expect you."

Or maybe they met whenever Giovanna and I were fighting. We'd certainly had our fights. And whenever we had a fight, Giovanna refused to spend the night with me. Sometimes lasted for days on end. Then everything was fine again, and we'd celebrate the end of hostilities in bed, after an intimate candlelight dinner. Business as usual in the life of any couple. Thinking back on our more recent quarrels, I found myself thinking that they occasionally seemed almost contrived. I had taken for granted that it was the stress over the impending wedding, but now that I thought about it, it was entirely possible that Giovanna had staged them in order to have an extra opportunity to see her secret lover. Giovanna wanted to break up with him, but he was trying to hold the relationship together. So she was obliged to see him more often, in order to persuade him to accept the end of their clandestine liaison. There is no question they had to meet at night, because it would be practically impossible for Giovanna to get away successfully during the day. Between the time she had to spend in the law office, in court, and with me, she didn't have a spare minute. We rarely ate lunch together, but Prunella had told me that she almost always came home for lunch. And during the day, the town has a thousand eyes, a thousand tongues. Giovanna's little town house was in a private and discreet neighborhood, but her lover certainly couldn't park out front. Her neighbors were accustomed to seeing my car parked there. He must have left his car in an adjoining street and then walked to her house. I thought of mentioning that point to Mele: maybe he should question the neighbors. It also occurred to me that the forensic office must have done some sloppy work if they had failed to find any traces of the murderer. Maybe I could find those traces. I knew Giovanna and perhaps I would know just where to look. Five minutes later, I was heading over to her house.

I did what I presumed her lover must have done, and parked my car in the parallel side street. Dogs barked as I walked past, but no one paid any attention. I opened the garden gate and walked up to the front door. I broke the seals of the district attorney's office, and I pulled my set of keys out of my overcoat pocket. I still had my keys because the detectives hadn't gotten around to confiscating them from me yet. A few seconds later, I was in the house. I made sure that the shutters were tightly fastened, and turned on the light.

I was torn between two emotions: sheer terror at the idea of being caught, and pure determination to find any evidence that would provide me with her lover's identity. The house was a mess, after the going-over that the Carabinieri had given it. There were splotches and smears of grey fingerprint powder everywhere. I found nothing. Finally, I gathered my courage and walked into the bedroom. I wanted to find out the truth about something that had been tormenting me from the moment I had discovered that my fiancée had a lover. What I was about to do was absolutely necessary: unless I resolved this, it would become an obsession. I swung open the twin doors of the large armoire and began rummaging through the drawers. I found my hands filled with Giovanna's lingerie; my fingers explored the light silky objects. I had purchased almost every item for her, in costly boutiques, in cities that were of course far away from our hometown. I had always been a lover of fine underthings. And Giovanna responded to this fantasy of mine. I liked watching her as she slowly undressed, removing her silk thigh-highs and her bra, and then slipping under the sheets next to me with nothing on but her panties. She wanted me to slip them off her, down her legs, but only at the last moment. In the days since the murder I had often wondered if she had offered herself to her lover wearing "my" lingerie. As I rummaged through the armoire, I hoped I would find different lingerie. And fortunately, one drawer yielded up the hoped-for trove of ordinary, unremarkable underthings. I felt a tremendous sense of relief. Giovanna might have betrayed me, but at least she had made sure to protect our little secret. Giovanna did love me after all.

I heard a muffled noise from downstairs. I immediately turned off the light and looked down over the railing. I was certain that it was the Carabinieri, and I racked my brain to come up with a plausible excuse. Then the cone of light from a flashlight illuminated the floor.

He came in the back door, I thought. In a split second I came to the conclusion that it must be the killer, and I hurtled down the stairs.

He heard me coming and pointed the flashlight straight into my eyes. A roar issued from my chest, and I lunged at him. We tumbled to the ground. I was shouting as I tried to hit him. He defended himself by clubbing me in the throat with his flashlight. It was a lucky blow, and it left me gasping.

He took advantage of my helplessness to get to his feet and shine the flashlight on me. I could hear him panting. I was trying to gather my strength to attack him again. He wouldn't get away from me.

The cone of light swiveled around, and I suddenly found myself looking at a drawn, creased face, framed by long dirty grey hair, pulled into a ponytail with a rubber band.

"It's me, Alvise Barovier," he said. "Giovanna's father."

My father invited me over to his house for dinner. He only did that when he had something important to tell me. Otherwise, we'd meet at Nevio, his favorite restaurant, a short distance from his law firm. It used to be a country inn, without any furnishings to speak of but with incredible cooking. The food was still first class, but an architect had transformed it into a horrible deluxe restaurant, with walls painted Venetian pink, and tables and chairs in the Parisian brasserie style. Papa's cook was good, too.

"Tagliolini in hot broth, assorted boiled meat with a side dish of peas and potato purée," the butler announced as he set the tureen on the table. "Nothing could be better when it's this cold."

Papa asked him to open a bottle of Merlot. It was from Selvaggia's wine cellars. The Conte Giannino, earlier than all the others, had grasped the potential of Venetian wines at a time when most of the local farmers produced low-quality vintages. He had hired a famous Piedmontese enologist. In just a few years' time his vineyard had established a national reputation for itself, and his wines were being praised in trade magazines. After his death, the Contessa had ignored the wine business, leaving all the details to the enologist and to Filippo, who wanted to carry on his father's work. Filippo had been very fond of his father.

"I talked to the district attorney," Papa announced, as he poured me a glass of wine. "He assured me that he will personally keep an eye on the investigation, though he's not going to replace Zan."

"Is that all?" I blurted out in disappointment.

"Zan will do his duty. Marchesin is a tough old nut, and he'll keep me posted on progress, so we can offer suggestions, too."

"I would have preferred a more talented prosecutor."

"That's the best I could do," he defended himself. "Problems with the internal workings of the local magistrature— these are problems we have to deal with on a daily basis in court."

"Mele hinted to me that he needs a longer leash, more freedom to take initiatives of his own."

He nodded his head. "Understood. I'll pass the message on to Marchesin."

I changed the subject. "Did Giovanna ever talk to you about her father's trial?"

"No. And I was glad to avoid the subject. That whole matter caused Giovanna a lot of pain, and I didn't want to open old wounds."

"She was certain that her father was innocent."

Papa looked at me in surprise. "Really? She told you so?"

"Once, a long time ago."

"I understand. Alvise was her father, but I was his defense lawyer and, unfortunately, I have to say that his guilt was unmistakable. He was loaded down with debt, the bank had turned off the faucets, and so he set fire to the furniture factory in order to lay his hands on the insurance money. As a result, the watchman and his wife were burned alive . . ."

"What was his defense?"

"The worst imaginable. He supplied a false alibi and forced me to put forward the theory of a plot carried out against him by mysterious enemies. With no evidence, without a single name. It was just pitiful. I took his case only because we were childhood friends and we had grown up together."

"What was he like?"

He shrugged. "A whoremonger and a gambler. In his personal life and in business. Why do you want to know?"

"I'm trying to put together the pieces of Giovanna's life. I'm trying to understand her. At the time, I was in boarding school, I didn't know what was happening. Maybe I've missed something important."

My father spooned a little horseradish sauce onto the breast of chicken on his plate. He sighed. "I'm worried about you, Francesco," he said. "You need to find the strength to strike back. Think of your future instead of torturing yourself like this."

"It's not easy."

"I know that. That's why it's important for you to come to work in the law firm as soon as possible." He cut a forkful of chicken and raised it to his mouth, studying my reaction as he did so. There was no reaction. "I shouldn't talk about it yet, but you are a future partner in the firm, as well as my son . . ." he continued in the voice he used in court to capture the attention of the court. "The Torrefranchi Foundation has decided to move the entire group out of the country. We are preparing an industrial site just outside of Timisoara, in Romania. All that will remain here are a few operations that are either distinctly local or very prestigious, like the wine production."

I gaped at him in astonishment. Papa had certainly succeeded in capturing my full and undivided attention. For the past year he had traveled frequently to Romania. He had told me that he was keeping track of cases for a few different clients. What he was really doing was organizing the wholesale transfer of the Foundation.

"Why?" I asked.

"The group is no longer competitive. High operating costs and too little investment in technological research and development. The Chinese are eating our lunch on a daily basis," he answered.

"What about the law firm?"

He smiled with satisfaction. "That's exactly what I wanted to talk to you about. In the early days, I'm going to have to spend a substantial part of my time in Timisoara, and I need someone to run the law firm while I'm gone." He pointed his fork at me. "I was planning to tell you about it when you got back from your honeymoon."

Just a few days earlier, I would have been overjoyed, but now I felt empty and listless. I shook my head. "I can't do it, Papa."

He wasn't giving up. "In two days I'm leaving for Timisoara. Why don't you come with me? A change of scenery would do you good."

I laid the fork and knife down on my plate. The time had come to say something important. "Before I take on something like that, I have to find out who killed Giovanna. I don't think I can go on living and working in this town without that knowledge. Do you understand what I'm trying to say?"

Papa nodded, seriously. "Understood. If that's how you feel about it, take all the time you need."

As soon as it was dark, I got into my car and drove until I turned down a dirt road. I pulled up outside an old mansion that was in ruins. Alvise Barovier stood in the open front door, smoking as he leaned against the jamb. He looked like a hobo. I followed him inside. He led me to a large room that must once have been a drawing room. Now it was decorated with a sofa that was shedding all its stuffing from various lacerations, sitting in front of a fireplace in which a fire burned merrily. He pointed to the sofa. I shook my head no. I didn't like him. The night before, after our tussle in Giovanna's house, he had jabbered out a disjointed story, most of which I had failed to understand. He had begged me to tell no one that he was in town. He promised to tell me everything, the next day. And now here I was, in that hovel, ready to listen.

"I don't know where to begin," he said uncomfortably.

"Why are you hiding? Why didn't you come to Giovanna's funeral?" I bore in on him harshly.

He threw more wood on the fire. "I don't want anyone to see me until I've uncovered the truth."

"Really," I replied ironically.

He looked hard at me. "Sit down, boy," he ordered. "I have a long story to tell you."

After he was released from prison, Alvise Barovier couldn't

come back to town. The guilty verdict and jail sentence had ruined him. Everyone had abandoned him. His relatives and the friends with whom he had sipped thousands of aperitifs, with whom he had played soccer as a boy, had all turned their backs. Even Prunella refused to so much as see him after his arrest. Only Giovanna had always believed in his innocence, but she was only a little girl. There was nothing she could do to help him. After traveling around Europe, he arrived in Argentina, like an Italian emigrant in the late nineteenth century. He had found work in a vineyard, near the city of Mendoza. The vineyard was owned by a family of Venetian origin. Over all those years, he stayed in sporadic contact with his daughter. The occasional Christmas card mailed in secret. Prunella refused to allow his name to be spoken under her roof. About six months earlier, he had received a phone call from Giovanna informing him that she had discovered the truth about the fire in the furniture factory. She had refused to say more, but his daughter was overjoyed. "They'll pay for what they did," she had said before hanging up. They had spoken on other occasions, and each time Giovanna was more confident and more determined. She had found proof that it was a plot, just as he had always claimed. Then, suddenly, she had stopped calling, and when he called her, Giovanna had been evasive. She had asked him to be patient. When the time was ripe, she'd get in touch with him. Instead, she had never called or written him again. And so he decided to return home, to discover the reason for her odd behavior. But the very same night he came back to town, Giovanna had been murdered.

"They wanted to keep her from talking," he said when he was done, his eyes swollen with tears.

"Giovanna was murdered by her lover, after a sexual encounter. That's the only truth. The sperm they found in her body proves it," I shot back in an unpleasant tone of voice.

"You don't believe me, do you?"

"No," I replied decisively. "And there was never any plot. You were guilty as hell."

"How can you be so sure?"

"My father told me. He also told me that you were a whore-monger and a gambler."

He smiled bitterly. "Good old Antonio. He never really tried to win my case. He was even embarrassed to be my defense lawyer."

"Your case was a lost cause from the outset. If you had just confessed, the court would have gone easy on you."

He seized the lapels of my coat. "I never did a thing. I'm innocent, do you hear me?"

I grabbed his wrists, freed myself from his grip, and stood up. "Don't get worked up. I don't care either way," I said flatly. "But I do want to know one thing: did Giovanna ever tell you she was getting married?"

"No."

"That's strange too, don't you think? She calls you repeatedly, but she never provides you with a single piece of evidence from the investigation to clear your name, and she even forgets to tell you that she was about to get married."

He shook his head dejectedly. "That's how it went."

"Go to the cemetery and put a flower on your daughter's grave. And show your face around town, nobody cares about that old story anymore. It doesn't make any sense for you to keep hiding, living like a hobo."

A nervous giggle issued from his chest. "I am a hobo. I can't be anything but a hobo here."

I turned and walked to the door. "I need your help," he begged. "I can't uncover the truth by myself."

I didn't even bother to answer. That man was just pathetic.

I went to Prunella's house. I hadn't found anything at the law firm or in Giovanna's house. Now I wanted to try Giovanna's old room in her mother's house. The investigators hadn't searched there yet. Maybe Zan didn't want to cause Prunella any new pain by searching her house. Or, more likely, he hadn't thought of it yet. I hoped she would be alone. I was lucky. She came to the door wearing a pair of old rubber gloves.

"I'm cleaning the silver," she explained.

On the kitchen table were a couple of pieces from an antique set of silverware. I wondered where the rest of the silver had gone. The radio was turned up high, and was tuned to the religious broadcaster, Radio Maria. "I was wondering if I could take a look at Giovanna's room," I said, "maybe there's something in there I'd like as a keepsake . . ."

"Sure, go right ahead."

It was still the room of an eighties teenager, with a few souvenirs from childhood. Her favorite doll and her old posters. There were no photographs of Alvise. I plunged into the netherworld of old memories, and I started poking around with a melancholy curiosity. On the desk was her digital camera. I turned it on, and the first image that appeared on the little screen showed Giovanna and me, smiling, wrapped in an embrace. A weekend in Paris, I recalled. I switched the camera off with a sigh, and I started pulling open drawers. I immediately found the file of documents from her father's trial. As I leafed through it, I realized that Giovanna had scribbled comments on various pages and had underlined certain names. In particular, she had underlined the name of Giacomo Zuglio, frequently, with a blue pencil. I was surprised. Giovanna shut herself up in that room to study the record of the trial. A lengthy and meticulous study, to judge from her notes. On the last page of the file I found a yellow sticky note: "Test samples. Remind Carla."

I slipped the digital camera into my pocket and the file under my arm. I couldn't wait to read it.

Carla Pisani lived in a recently built apartment house on the edge of town, a hundred yards from the railroad tracks. Not far off was the industrial area that had been built a dozen years ago. The one that sprang up after the war was in the opposite direction, by the river. It was nine in the morning on a Sunday, and I was sure that I would find her at thome. The architect had clearly meant to make the three-story apartment building resemble an old granary, newly renovated. The dish antennas on the roof, however, gave quite a different impression. As I walked up to the front door, I met a young woman pushing a stroller. The child swathed in a red down playsuit waved hello to me with one little hand.

The mother recognized me immediately. "I used to see your fiancée here often," she said. "She would come to see Carla. I'm sorry about what happened."

I gave her the standard sad smile. I no longer had the patience to listen to useless chatter.

"Carla's not in," she told me. "I saw her leave ten minutes ago, on her bicycle."

"You don't know where she went, do you?"

"She generally goes out for breakfast at the café, and to buy the morning newspapers. She should be back soon."

I got back in my car and drove around, looking for her. I saw her bicycle leaning against the wall of an old building that housed a *latteria*, a milk bar. Actually, the latteria was long gone. All that remained was the sign. Now it was an absolutely standard Italian small-town café and tobacco shop, and most of the customers were factory workers from the adjoining industrial area. When I was a boy, I used to come to this latteria often during the summer. The woman who ran the place made excellent fruit frappes. My favorite was the sour black cherry frappe. I parked outside and went in. Aside from a couple of drunks who were sipping their first shot of hard liquor, the only customer was Carla. She was seated at a little café table, reading the newspaper. The barista stepped around from behind the counter to serve her a cappuccino and a pastry.

"An espresso with a little steamed milk," I ordered.

When Carla heard my voice, she lowered the newspaper she was reading and stared hard at me. "I thought you only frequented the piazza café," she said sarcastically. "This is hardly up to your usual level."

I ignored her and sat down across from her. "What do you want?" she asked in a serious tone of voice.

I pulled the yellow sticky note out of my pocket and placed it in front of her. "What does this mean?"

"Nothing you'd be interested in."

"Fine. I'll take it to Inspector Mele. He'll be sure to come ask you about it."

Carla turned pale. "No, don't do it."

"Then answer my question."

"Who else has seen it?"

"No one else. But what's all the mystery about?"

She bit her lip. She pulled a pack of cigarettes out of the pocket of her heavy jacket. Then she remembered that she couldn't smoke indoors and cursed under her breath.

"Well?" I insisted.

Carla didn't answer. She seemed frightened.

"I didn't kill Giovanna. You have to believe me," I said quietly and very calmly. "I want to find out who did. If you know something, you have to tell me."

Carla tore open a sugar packet and poured it into her cappuccino. She slowly stirred it. Then she bit into her pastry.

"Frozen. It's disgusting!" she blurted out. "There was a time when cafés got their pastries from local shops. Those were real pastries. Nowadays, they buy them by the bag, frozen, and pop them into the microwave. Just so they can earn an extra euro here and there."

I nodded in agreement. Carla was stalling to try to figure out if she could trust me. I decided not to push her. My espresso was served, and I gulped it down.

"Even the milk is different now," I said. "It used to taste of hay."

"Giovanna didn't like it."

"She couldn't even stand the smell of milk. She drank fruit juice for breakfast."

"Pear juice."

"Or lately, mixed carrot juice, other things like that."

She stared at me yet again. "I didn't kill her," I repeated.

She pulled her coin purse out of her handbag and paid for breakfast. "Let's go," she said.

After about ten minutes of driving she told me to stop the car. Until then she had only uttered terse instructions on which way to turn.

"Get out," she said.

We were parked by the river bank. She pointed to an irrigation canal that flowed into the river through a huge cement pipe that ran through the levee that formed the river bank here from one side to the other. Then she gestured to me, and set off. I followed her. We walked through the fields for ten minutes or so, following the line of the canal; then we climbed to the top of a low hill. My shoes and the legs of my trousers were spattered with mud. I still didn't understand the point of that hike through the countryside, but I was afraid to ask any questions. I was afraid she would change her mind.

When we got to the top, Carla stopped and pointed to an enclosed area, surrounded by high walls topped with barbed wire. Aside from a couple of large dogs running back and forth inside the walls, it seemed deserted.

"That's where they hide it," she said.

"What?"

"The toxic waste."

"What on earth are you talking about?" I asked impatiently.

Carla lit a cigarette. She took a deep drag and then, finally, decided to talk.

Giovanna had called her a year ago. Carla had just broken up with her fiancé. He had persuaded her to move down to Caserta with him; now Giovanna asked her if she wanted to come back to live in the Northeast. Carla told her she was willing, there was no longer anything to keep her down south in Campania. She wanted to start over in new surroundings. Giovanna found her a job in town, at the local health board as a lab technician. Carla was happy with her new situation; she couldn't have asked for anything better. Her mother was happy too. After her husband had died, she was alone in the world, and it was a consolation to have her daughter living nearby. As soon as she returned to town, though, Carla understood that Giovanna hadn't helped her to return home out of friendship alone. She wanted something in exchange. And she told Carla so in no uncertain terms. She suspected that there was a massive fraud involving the disposal of industrial wastes, and she was pretty sure that a number of officials of the local health board were implicated. According to Giovanna's plans, Carla would try to investigate from within. Carla didn't want to do it. Giovanna took it pretty hard, and to save their friendship, Carla agreed to keep her eyes wide open and her ears to the ground. At the local health board, she hadn't discovered anything solid, but a sudden fish kill reported by some fishermen a couple of months earlier had persuaded her to do some tests on the water. The fish had been poisoned by chromium and other substances that had washed into the river from the canal that we'd walked along before climbing the hill.

"The tests that Giovanna was waiting for had to do with several soil samples that I had dug up around the fence," she explained. "There is no doubt, the chemical substances come from that dirt, and the lot is nothing other than an illegal dump for toxic waste. Giovanna was right. The fraud exists, and it's well organized."

"Why didn't you report this to the Carabinieri?"

"I used the laboratory secretly, the very same night that Giovanna was killed. After that, I had other things on my mind."

"How does the fraud work?"

"It's really very simple. Instead of disposing of the waste as required by law, the companies save money by handing it over to unscrupulous individuals who get rid of it. No questions asked."

"And why was Giovanna investigating this fraud?"

"I don't know why," she replied, crumpling up her empty packet of cigarettes. "She wouldn't tell me, but I think it had something to do with her father's case."

"Alvise? How did he fit in?"

Carla pointed to the walled-in area with a quick flick of her hand. "That's where his furniture factory once stood. You know, the one that burned down."

I thought it over. Alvise had told me the truth. Giovanna was digging into the old story, and somehow she had found a link with the toxic waste fraud.

"Alvise is here," I told her.

"Really?" she exclaimed in surprise.

"He's hiding in an abandoned villa," I added. "He believes that Giovanna was killed to keep her from uncovering the plot that sent him to prison."

Carla shook her head skeptically. "I don't know. It's possible."

"Giovanna was killed by her lover. It was a crime of passion," I pointed out. Carla nodded, with a trace of sadness in her eyes. "Take me to Alvise. I want to meet him."

* * *

Hush, little baby, little baby of mine
I'll stitch you a smock of cambric fine.
I'll stitch it with thread of pink and of white
To your bride I will give it, 'twill be her delight.

It was the only nursery rhyme that Filippo could remember.

His aunt Adelina, his father's sister, used to sing it to him; she was an elderly woman, and he remembered the way she smelled of vanilla, as well as the crocheted shawl she used to pull around her shoulders to ward off the chill of old age.

Of his early childhood with his mother, however, all that he could recall was the sensation of her lifting him up to hand him over to grandma, a ritual that was repeated every evening. She had never spent time with him, reading him fairytales or pretending to sleep to lull him into slumber. She had always been dressed in an evening gown; she was always impeccably elegant.

That was the image that he was trying to shape in wax. The image of an unattainable woman.

It had taken a lot of insistence to persuade her to model for him. His mother had understood that there was a sarcastic edge to that request. Selvaggia used to model for the students of the Venice Academy of Fine Arts.

She understood that with his sculpture, Filippo wanted to remind her of who and what she had once been.

Moreover, all that gouging with a red-hot iron into a wax face that was beginning to resemble her in an unsettling fashion was making her feel quite uneasy.

Once she had tried to change his mind about using wax, suggesting that he do a plaster bust of her, but he had mischievously explained that plaster wasn't suitable, that it was an unrefined material, and that for plaster first you had to use a clay model which, after the moulding, had to be split in two. And that he didn't think he could bring himself to split her head in two.

egretted
ith con-

n a week
undation,

d later. He
mnia was his

ight Giovanna
home. He had
orced to go look for

wasn't there. She finally
arrived at dawn.

When he told her about his fight with Francesco she had
flown into a rage, and had ordered him to forget about Giovanna. Then she had given him his usual cocktail of tranquilizers.

Neither of them could get to sleep, and so they wound up
playing pinochle until lunchtime. They hadn't spoken again,
looking one another in the eye only when it was the other
one's turn to play. There was the usual silence full of tacit
allusions that had built up over the years, and underscored
by the snapping of the cards that his mother shuffled like a
professional.

But not tonight. Tonight we have to talk. When will she be
here? he wondered, overwhelmed with anxiety.

An hour later he heard the sound of tires on gravel.

He had built his studio on the ground floor so he could
keep on eye on her comings and goings.

The sensation that his mother was trying to elude his sur-
veillance drove him crazy.

"Who were you with?" he asked her as soon as she
appeared at the door to his studio.

"The usual friends," she answered laconically.

"Who?" he insisted.

Selvaggia puffed out her cheeks in annoyance. She tossed her bag on an armchair and took off her evening coat. She was as elegant as Nefertiti and her cleavage demanded the attention of any man older than twenty.

As she removed her Cartier earrings, she poured forth the list of friends like a schoolteacher with a migraine performing the enormously tiresome task of taking attendance.

"Tormene, Cesaretto, Ostan, Judge Morbelli . . ."

"That's fine," said Filippo with a note of hysteria in his voice. He stood up and grabbed the cordless phone.

"Let's give them a call."

"What are you doing, have you lost your mind? Put down that telephone. You can't call people up at this time of night!"

They had battled for the phone. Filippo held it hidden behind his back, and in order to grab it out of his hands, Selvaggia was forced to wrap her arms around him in an embrace.

Filippo looked into her green cat's eyes. No one could hope to resist that gaze. He let the cordless phone fall to the floor and held her arms firmly.

"Who are you seeing now?"

She boldly refused to answer.

He grabbed her by the wrists.

"I'm still young, I have every right to have fun . . ."

"With who?"

"Let me go," she said as she broke free of his grasp. As she rubbed her wrists, she murmured:

"Davide Trevisan."

"Davide Trevisan! I went to school with him. He's my age, do you realize that?"

"I don't have to ask anyone's permission, least of all yours."

"Papa would turn over in his grave if he knew."

"Oh spare me, your father! All he knew how to do was

* * *

For the second time in two days, I was going back to Prunella's house. I had something important I wanted to ask her. Alvise had left his country hovel, and had moved into Carla's apartment. At first he resisted the idea, but Carla had insisted, after promising him that she would help him in his investigation. Even though it had been years since they had spoken, they had hugged warmly the first time. Carla, too, had always believed he was innocent.

"I knew him well," she told me in the car. "He loved that furniture factory. He would never have set fire to it."

"He was over his head in debt. Gambling debts," I shot back.

Carla lit a cigarette. "He would have sold it. He wasn't stupid enough to attempt such a clumsy piece of fraud."

I apologized to Alvise. He had told the truth on least one point: Giovanna had pulled out the trial record and studied it carefully and thoroughly. She really was a fine lawyer. Carla told him the rest of the story. The news that the land where his furniture factory had once stood was now a secret toxic waste dump left him speechless. He picked up a two-liter bottle of red wine and took a long, gulping swig.

"Once there was a fine factory on that land, now it's a fucking toxic waste dump," he commented bitterly. "Before the trial, I had put all my property in Prunella's name, to avoid losing everything in damages in case I was convicted. At least on that point your father was farsighted."

And now I was on my way to see his ex-wife to ask for information about the land. She wasn't actually his ex, to tell the truth. Alvise and Prunella had never divorced. For her, it was a sacrilege to break the sacred bond of matrimony.

When I parked outside the front gate, Prunella came to meet me with a rake in her hands.

"Gardeners cost a fortune nowadays," she said, as if to justify herself. "I was just going in to have a cup of tea. Would you like to join me?"

"No, thanks," I answered hastily. "I only have one question for you: what did you do with the land where the furniture factory stood?"

Prunella's face darkened. "I sold it. About three years ago. I have nothing else, you know? Just this home. And I don't know how I can ever keep it up in the years to come."

"If you need money, just ask. Papa and I are at your disposal."

"I'm not used to asking for charity. To think that we were once the wealthiest family in town. That damned Alvise managed to squander a fortune in just a few years."

"There's still Giovanna's house and bank account," I reminded her, annoyed by her squalid concerns.

"When the courts free up the estate. That'll take a long time."

"Papa could help you with that. I'll mention it to him," I

"That hair made him look older," she explained.

"Well?" Alvise asked.

I said the name. Barovier leapt to his feet and snatched the towel away from his neck. "Zuglio, that bastard son of a bitch," he snarled. "He was the bank officer who destroyed my business. I had a contract to manufacture furniture for a chain of hotels in Turkey. It was two solid years of production, but he cut off my line of credit, out of the blue, and demanded all the money back. It was a knockout blow. I couldn't find any other banks willing to help. My friends wouldn't help either, for that matter."

"Do you think that Zuglio was involved in the plot to send you to prison?" Carla asked.

"I'm sure of it. He made the first move, to establish a motive."

I said nothing. I could easily have refuted the statement, but why bother? Alvise, however, noticed my silence.

"You don't believe me, do you?"

I spread my arms helplessly. "I have a hard time believing there was a plot. Who would have a reason to ruin you?"

Alvise started walking back and forth in the room. "I don't think you can imagine how often I've thought about it. It was a difficult time, lots of things were changing, but it was possible to glimpse the dawn of the golden age of the Northeast. Conte Giannino and I were planning to create an organized industrial sector."

"Exactly what the Torrefranchi Foundation did later," I broke in.

"Precisely. There weren't many companies back then and we didn't really know what we were doing, but we did know that we could consolidate and coordinate our operations. And we knew that would make us stronger, both on the market and as an association. It was our dream. Instead, I wound up in prison, and he died of a heart attack a short while later."

He sat back down, his gaze lost in an indeterminate moment in the past. Barovier was a beaten man dreaming pointlessly of redemption. I felt no pity for him. He had squandered his fortune on roulette; he had betrayed his wife—details that vanished from his version of what happened. Carla wrapped the towel around his neck again and went back to cutting his hair, with a cigarette clamped between her lips. Between the index and middle fingers of her left hand, she would seize a lock of hair, check the length, and then clip it. The smoke from her cigarette forced her to close one eye, but she didn't seem to mind. Only when the cigarette had burned down to the filter did she finally decide to stub it out. She reached out for an ashtray emblazoned with the logo of a pharmaceutical company.

"Zuglio ruined the Barovier family's life," Carla said suddenly, staring at me.

I immediately saw what she was driving at. I had thought of it myself. "I became the slut of the man who ruined my life," that damned sentence that I couldn't get out of my mind was beginning to make sense. Moreover, Zuglio's name

"I know him by sight," I said. "I can assure you that he's not Giovanna's type."

"What do you know?" Alvise cried. "Maybe Giovanna got caught up in something she couldn't control."

"Maybe she didn't know how to manage things properly," Carla added. "She got in over her head, and wound up in bed with that bastard."

"You're fantasizing now," I replied, uncertainly. "Anyway, all we know about Zuglio is what they say about him in town."

"We can always find out the rest," Alvise suggested.

* * *

Giacomo Zuglio was a short man. Until third grade, he had been the tallest kid in his class. Then all the other kids that he had enjoyed tormenting began to grow, leaving him behind and, finally, looking down at him from above. From then on, the fun was over for him. His only purpose was to clamber over obstacles that cropped up in his path, each of them always too tall to get over easily. It was hard for him; by nature he was a fighter, a puncher, a combatant.

He'd had to settle for a bank job. When he was hired, he was convinced that he had what it takes for a spectacular career, but that's not how it went. He remained on the ground floor, a humble director of a small-town branch. Any jerk could look down on him, just because he was so-and-so or such-and-such, from this important family, descended from this or that successful manufacturer. Lawyers, doctors, industrialists, craftsmen: they were all better than him. Soon, however, he noticed that there was a river of money flowing through his little branch of the bank, and not all of that money was earned through sheer hard work. And so he began to use the bank as if it were his personal property. He loaned money at cutthroat rates and deposited the profits in his personal coffers, which took the form of a fictitious holding company, a shell company that he had founded under his wife's name. Once he had socked away enough money to equal a sizable win at the state lottery, he resigned from the bank and began his career as an "investor."

His masterpiece had been a three-million euro swindle, the "Klondike gold rush." He had got in touch with certain Italo-Canadians, well known to the FBI and Scotland Yard since the seventies, who turned out to be the owners of a few gold mines in Canada.

There actually was a little bit of gold still in them, but it would cost too much to bring it to the surface.

He had enrolled twenty or so fake promoters, genuine talents in the realm of cajoling and tricking the gullible and simple-minded. He had put together conventions in luxury hotels run by his usual group of friends and he had printed up tempting prospectuses. There was even a video depicting the bustling activity at the mine site.

The fraud had scooped up the savings of about a thousand

out of it. People from the Northeast refuse to listen to reason; they think that by investing 3,500 euros they can earn 21,900 euros. The most mistrustful investors were invited to Canada. There they were welcomed by attractive hostesses, loaded into limousines, and then accompanied to the mines, where work was proceeding at a furious pace. When they returned home, they told their friends what they had seen, and they ultimately proved to be even more persuasive than the salesmen.

Zuglio had never shown his face to the investors. Once he had the money in hand, he paid off the salesmen, gave them time to get far away, and then reported the fraud to the police, making it appear that his own financial holding company had been the chief victim of those Canadian bastards.

After that swindle, he devoted his time to less fanciful but more remunerative activities: loan sharking, buying and selling real estate, and money laundering.

He had learned to operate discreetly; he frequented the same businessmen who, on occasion, saw their companies staggered beneath the burden of his 300 percent rate of interest. They continued to look down on him, but his diminutive stature no longer put them in a jocular mood. He owned fine homes and expensive automobiles. He could afford beautiful women of every race and color. He had even started investing in art. But he still wasn't enjoying himself. There was only one thing that could brighten his world: to be allowed into the circle that mattered, the circle of the Torrefranchi Foundation.

He needed to rise to those heights. Only then could he feel that he had achieved his dream.

With the smile of a man who is certain that he will succeed, Zuglio parked in front of the town's leading real estate agency. He got out of the car and opened the trunk of the Ferrari 612 Scaglietti that he had just purchased for himself. In the trunk were three rigid briefcases.

Before entering the building, Zuglio pulled a for-sale sign off the plate glass window: PRESTIGIOUS HISTORIC TOWNHOUSE. VILLA DISTRICT. PRICE NEGOTIABLE.

Eliana Dal Toso, the bottle blonde who ran the real estate agency, came toward him, her eyes already glittering. Women like being blonde, but they don't understand that brunettes light more fires, he thought indifferently. And her mouth was tight, and as everyone knows, like mouth like pussy.

In other words, the girl left him cold, which always made business dealings a little simpler and more effective.

The contract was ready and waiting. Zuglio signed it without a second glance, because he knew no one would dare to cheat him, handed over the valise, and ripped up the for-sale sign. In a couple of months, he'd resell the villa at twice the price. There was already interest from a Hollywood movie star. Now that Tuscany and Lake Como were well known, the jetset had discovered the Palladian villas. In his opinion, living in the countryside was nothing but a pain in the ass. All those mosquitoes . . .

declared bankruptcy, but the
practically had a stroke. Not so long as there was a breath
in his body—and so forth. As a result, his son turned to the
banks, and then, when his line of credit was used up, he turned
to Zuglio, a midget cash machine who made loans at interest
rates that started at twenty percent, and then rose to forty percent. Today's loan would be the last. Billiard Ball would never
be able to pay back the two hundred thousand euros contained
in the second valise and Zuglio would become the owner of a
nice little factory.

The second meeting was over in less time than the first,
and Zuglio had to smile when he saw that bald head leaning
forward, in a bow like that of a condemned man about to be
guillotined.

It was 11 in the morning, the day had barely begun. He still
had to swing by to meet with Prunella Barovier, another citizen
who no longer had two pennies to rub together. She had asked
him to lend her fifteen thousand euros so that she could bury
her whore of a daughter in high style. He had agreed to lend
her the money at a ridiculous rate of interest, just for the pleas-

ure of watching her sob and blow snot into the last handker-chief with stitched monograms that she owned.

But first he needed to fill the tank with gas: that fucking Ferrari 612 got worse mileage than an American Hummer.

The espresso that the widow Barovier offered him was dis-gusting. He took a tiny sip and then left it to grow cold next to the pile of banknotes that he was counting out under the eyes of Prunella.

"Fourteen thousand eight hundred . . . and nine hundred, fifteen thousand," he finished counting, rubbing each bill between thumb, middle finger and index finger.

"I don't know when I'll be able to pay you back."

"Don't let that bother you, you'll pay me when you can. You made a sacrifice, but your daughter deserves a worthy farewell. Unfortunately, the people who run the funeral homes are shameless profiteers."

The bundle of cash sat on the table. Neither of them seemed to want to touch it, as if it didn't exist. You're disgust-ed by money, but as soon as I leave you'll scoop it up with both hands, Zuglio thought, as he paid lip service to his condo-lences. The poor little hypocrite was sitting on the very edge of her chair. It was obvious that she couldn't wait to get him out of the house. Unfortunately for her, he had plenty of time to waste that day. He also had an offer to make. He was just cast-ing around for the best approach.

"There's something I've been meaning to ask you for years," he began. "Well . . . I never had anything against your husband. Unfortunately, back then, as the president of the bank, I was forced to cut off his line of credit."

"Don't think twice. So much time has passed since then."

She must have practiced for years the art of the kind of for-giveness that makes you feel like a shit. But her confessional tone wouldn't work with him. He looked around carefully, noticing the traces of neglect, the water stains, the shadows of said as he stood up.

"That was more than evident," the widow Barovici ... drily, as she raised an arm to point him toward the exit.

Anyway, he'd baited the hook and tossed it. It was only a matter of time now. Only a matter of accumulating interest.

* * *

The hall of the Order of Attorneys on the second floor of the court building was crowded with lawyers. I arrived at the last minute and had to push my way through the crowd to make it to my seat in the front row. On the low stage that had been set up for the occasion, there was a chair draped with a lawyer's robes. They were Giovanna's robes. When my father stepped up onto the stage, the hall fell silent. He was ashen and drawn.

"Beloved colleagues," he began, in a solemn tone. "As chairman of the Order, it is customarily my sad duty to commemorate those who are no longer among us. And yet I never expected to have to honor the memory of the youngest colleague at the bar: Giovanna Barovier. Giovanna joined my law firm as an intern and never left. I admired her skill and intelligence, and I was very fond of her. She was about to marry my son, Francesco. But today, I am obliged to recall the life of the legal professional who once wore these robes . . ."

My father choked up; he couldn't finish the sentence. He covered his face with both hands, sobbing.

"Excuse me," he whispered.

Then he fell to his knees. The microphone emitted a whistle. I hurried to the lectern, along with everyone in the front row.

"I'm sorry," he mumbled. "I'll be all right in a minute."

"Forget about it, Antonio," said one of his colleagues. "Just go home."

"He's right," I said, as I helped him to his feet. "There's nothing more to say."

We walked out of the hall, flanked by two lines of lawyers. Some of them had expressions of profound sympathy and emotion on their faces, others had a glint of cruel satisfaction in their eyes. Papa's success had always fostered rancor and envy, and there were more than a few for whom the sight of Antonio Visentin down on his knees, sobbing pitifully, must have been a priceless source of gratification.

My father refused to forgive himself. I walked him back to his offices. The secretaries had already been alerted about what had happened, and they overwhelmed him with attention, although in the inimitably discreet style that was a hallmark of the Visentin law firm.

"What an embarrassment," my father mumbled, as he sank into an office chair.

"You should have let another member of the order make the speech. Someone who was less emotionally involved."

"It was my responsibility."

I poured a glass of tonic water for him, let him calm down, and then I asked, "When are you leaving for Romania?"

"He..." he replied. "I

"A truck made a coup...
a driver and another guy. They unloaded some di...
one of them started up the excavator and buried them."

"It looks like Carla was right," I commented. "The next time they show up, we'll try to follow them. Maybe we can figure out where the toxic waste is coming from."

Alvise was numb with the cold. I suggested he sit in my car while I kept watch, but he refused. I would have preferred that he accept; that way I wouldn't have to stand around and make conversation. I didn't feel like talking. What I wanted was to go back home and climb into bed with a couple of Giovanna's sleeping pills in my belly, to erase from my mind the image of my father on his knees before his assembled colleagues. I had never seen him look so weak and fragile. Until then, he had always played the part of the strong man, capable of controlling his own feelings. But Giovanna's death had shaken him deep down, and in the end, it had been too much for him. I looked over at Alvise, as he stood surveying the lots with a pair of binoculars, wondering if I'd ever see him on his knees, broken by grief and pain. I couldn't bring myself to trust that man.

He was certain that Giovanna had been killed to keep her from rehabilitating his reputation. The very idea made me seethe with rage and jealousy. I was by no means confident that Alvise Barovier was worth such a sacrifice.

"Look, the truck is coming back," he said suddenly, handing me the binoculars.

Through the twin lenses I saw a man leap down from the cab of the truck to open the padlocked gate. The truck pulled in and he quickly swung the gate closed. The two dogs ran to greet him, tails wagging, and he leaned over to pat them. The driver pulled the truck further in and then stepped out of the cab. He climbed up onto the seat of the excavator and lifted the toothed bucket of the backhoe up to the cargo deck of the truck. After he had dropped the second drum into a pit in the dirt, I decided that I had seen enough. We hurried over to the car and prepared to follow the truck.

We watched as the truck pulled out of the dump and drove off toward town. It stopped in front of a café. The two got out and went inside long enough to drink an espresso, and then they continued on toward the new industrial district. The truck turned in through the opening front gate of a printing plant, the Grafica Santi & Giustinian. Ten minutes later, the truck was already barreling down the main road, heading back to the dump. There the two men unloaded a number of plastic jerry cans, which they buried in another pit.

"Tell me about Giovanna," said Alvise, breaking the silence that had endured until that moment.

"I'm not sure I feel like it."

"Why not?"

"Because the Giovanna I knew is a memory that I do not intend to share with anyone. Much less with you," I answered flatly. "You'll have to be satisfied with what we may discover by following those two trucks, like a couple of deranged investigators."

"You're stupid and arrogant," he said in an unemotional

"His name is Constantin Deaconescu. He came three or four years ago. He owns a nightclub."

"A pimp," Barovier commented. "What is the link between him and those drums filled with toxic waste?"

I didn't have the slightest idea. I was baffled. I had expected a simpler story. I kept watching the Romanian while he talked to the two truck drivers. He was dressed expensively but without taste or discernment. He lit a cigarette and offered the pack to the others. He was calm, relaxed. He certainly had no idea he was being spied on.

I passed the binoculars to Alvise. "I may not know that man," he said a few minutes later. "But I can say one thing for certain: he's a dangerous criminal."

"Pearls of wisdom, available at bargain rates?" I joked mockingly.

He sighed in annoyance. "Try spending a few years in prison, you'll learn to recognize gangsters," he explained. "And I can assure you that the Romanian is one of the really bad guys."

I turned the key in the ignition and started the car. I didn't have much experience with criminals. I was a corporate lawyer. I had been involved in only a few criminal cases, and they'd always been purse-snatchers or drug addicts who'd been caught stealing car radios.

"Maybe we should go have a chat with Inspector Mele."

"Not so fast, boy," he said in an insolent tone of voice. "We just need to be more careful. Now take me to Carla's house. I'm hungry."

Before getting out, he clapped a hat on his head and pulled up the collar of his jacket. I assume he meant it as a way to keep the neighbors from recognizing him. I doubted that anyone would remember his face after such a long time. If anything, he had rendered himself so shady and suspicious-looking that anyone would have noticed him and wondered what he was up to. He didn't bother to say goodbye. Which was just as well. I didn't feel like talking to him either.

* * *

"What shall we talk about today?" asked Eriberto Moroncini.

"Your ficus benjamin plant," Filippo answered. "You're taking bad care of it; it's not getting enough light."

Filippo was stretched out on a leather couch that was straight out of a movie. Everything was filmic in Moroncini's office. Especially the wainscoting. The use of a well-established stereotype, the renowned psychiatrist had explained in an interview in *Vogue*, helped to reassure patients about the reliability of the therapy. "Do you like plants?"

"I wish I had been born a plant. I could live on just light and water."

Moroncini scribbled with his black-and-green Parker pen a personal ideogram in his Moleskine notebook.

Filippo turned to look at him. "So you liked that one, eh?"

Moroncini remained expressionless. "Why plants?"

...while, but they're growing upward, reach-

Moron...

"Because my mother asked you to, that's ...y.

Moroncini closed his notebook.

"No one can say no to her, so you can imagine how hard it is for me," Filippo continued.

"Why, in your opinion?" This time, it wasn't a routine question.

Filippo stroked the leaves of the ficus benjamin with one finger.

"My mother is a power artist. Dominating other people is what excites her."

"And you? What excites you?"

"I'm impotent, didn't my mother tell you that?"

"She told me that you have a strong tendency toward self-pity."

Filippo started clapping in an ostentatious burst of applause.

"Fine. At last, a little stern orthodoxy."

"Are you sure that you're impotent? It seems to me that you've had a lot of girlfriends."

"Before I decided to give up sex, I was dating Giovanna Barovier. In the summer, we used to go to Forte dei Marmi. We have a turn-of-the-century villa there. Fifteen bedrooms. And you want to know something? I made sure we stayed in a hotel. Never at my house. My mother didn't like Giovanna, and she didn't give a damn whether I liked her."

"You could have gone somewhere else, you could taken a trip somewhere . . ."

"When you're born in a town like this, there's no way out, you can't even run away from someone you don't like. In a big city, if you don't like someone, you don't even have to tell them. Just don't take their phone calls."

"Who's keeping you from moving away? You're an adult, you're wealthy, you can do what you want."

"All I can do is what my mother wants."

"That depends entirely on you."

"Right. Which takes us back to square one."

* * *

A couple of days later, Carla phoned to invite me to dinner. From her tone, I understood that she had something important to tell me.

"Why don't you come over to my place?" I suggested. "I really don't want to see your house guest."

I had to insist, but Carla finally accepted, and now I was waiting for her, while keeping an eye on the simmering chopped onions and vegetables for the risotto. Carla arrived with a bottle of wine, a South African Cabernet Sauvignon.

"For once, no Calchi Renier wines," she joked.

She took off her ankle-length down overcoat. Underneath, she was wearing a dress with a simple cut. Her face was only slightly made up, and she was much cuter than usual. I felt guilty for thinking it.

The risotto wasn't bad. It was the first time I'd put any effort into cooking something since Giovanna's death.

"I～ ~h~+ ~ll~" C~rl~ ~~k~d ~~ I took the dirty plates into the

~~~~~ & ~~~~~~~~ p~~~~~ ~ ~ ~~ ~ ~~
a local company, the Eco T.D.W.—the T.D.W. stands for ecological treatment and disposal of waste."

"Instead they wound up in the secret dump."

"Right. The Eco T.D.W. is supposed to transform the waste into harmless, inert material, for use in building or agriculture, depending on which chemical substances are being treated."

"Do you know who owns it?"

Carla shook her head.

"Tomorrow I'll go to the Chamber of Commerce," I said. "It shouldn't be hard to find out."

"The checks are carried out by local health board staff," she explained as she rummaged through her purse for a pack of cigarettes. "I managed to get a look at the file for the printing plant. Everything seems to be in order. The signature belongs to a certain Arturo Ferrari, the director of the laboratory."

"I know him. The court has him do expert investigations from time to time."

"But he can't be the only corrupt official," Carla pointed out. "He must have accomplices in the regional government too."

"I wouldn't be surprised. The fraud must be profitable enough to grease all the wheels that need oiling."

Carla stood up and went over to pour herself a small shot of grappa. I couldn't help but remember that Giovanna couldn't stand grappa. She liked whiskey. A bottle of her favorite brand still stood on the tray.

Carla sniffed her liquor. "I've thought at length about this thing, and there's something that still doesn't make sense to me," she said. "The dump can't be the final destination for the toxic waste."

"What do you mean?"

"It's too close to town, don't you see? It doesn't make sense to bury it in your own backyard. They used to do it, but after a series of scandals and trials, they wised up."

"That quarry," I remembered. "Some of the kids who went to play in it developed tumors."

"And they all died," she pointed out. "I'm certain that they take the waste somewhere else."

"Maybe out of the country," I suggested, thinking of Constantin.

"Or to southern Italy," Carla suggested. "It's a gold mine for the Camorra. I learned about it when I worked in Caserta."

It was my turn to pour myself a shot of liquor. I chose a cognac.

"What did you find out about Zuglio?" my dinner guest asked.

"I've made some discreet inquiries myself. Zuglio lends money; according to rumors he's a loan shark, operating outside the law. Anyway, I found out the most important thing. He still owns that land. He never sold it or rented it."

"Then he's definitely involved in the fraud," Carla commented as she slipped into her down overcoat. She pulled a hat and woolen gloves out of the pocket.

At the door, she apologized for her suspicions. "I was

operation.

It was cocktail hour when I walked into the Bar Centrale. Davide, as always, was leaning on the counter with a wine spritzer in his hand. With his usual casual tone, he was recounting a piece of defamatory gossip about a woman who owned a local pet shop, and who was commonly nicknamed the "dick-breaker" because, for the second time now, one of her lovers had wound up at the emergency room with a "fractured" penis as a result of the unusual sexual practices that the woman demanded. Moreover, the guy in question was a well-known rugby player. Before going over to say hello, I waited for the laughter triggered by Davide's story to die down.

"I wanted to apologize," I told him right away. "I was upset after my fight with Filippo."

He extended his hand. "You're a good guy," he said with a smile. "What'll you drink?"

We chatted about this and that, then I managed to shift the conversation to the subject of work.

"How's it going with the threshing machines?" I asked.

He waved one hand in the air. "Oh, I got out of that business a while ago," he answered. "I wasn't making any money. Nowadays, aside from the vineyards, there's no agriculture around here. Just industrial sheds. Now I'm a *scoassaro*, a garbage collector."

"What do you mean?"

"I have an industrial waste company," he explained. "The regional government was offering funding, and I took advantage of the situation . . ."

I ordered another round of aperitifs. "And how's business?"

"It's going great," he said, making a rather vulgar gesture to ward off misfortune. Then he lowered his voice. "The great thing is that running this company got me into the Foundation as a member; I take care of waste disposal for every company in the group. So now I'm finally a member of the country club, and it's a paradise—all the hottest babes in the district."

"You're a member of the Foundation?" I repeated in disbelief.

"You didn't know? Your father was a big help. Though I have to say, Jesus God, his fees are something to behold . . . in my next life, I swear, I'm going to be a lawyer."

Trevisan continued to spout nonsense, but I wasn't listening to him anymore. I thought about my father. That miserable scoundrel Davide could ruin him if the fraud was uncovered.

And to think that we'd been friends since we were boys. I felt as if I'd been betrayed. Again.

That evening Carla called me. "So, any news?" she asked.

"Nothing," I lied. "It's going to take a few days. I'll call you as soon as I learn something."

I had no other options. I had to wait for Papa to come home and take care of the situation before it became public. Otherwise, the scandal would ruin him.

* * *

...ished was lit up like a spaceship, and a

...the Che...

blow the take from the last few robberies an...

They parked the off-road vehicle in a strategic location, and then elbowed and pawed their way onto the improvised dance floor, in the midst of a human wave that surged and subsided like so many flocks of panicky birds. They had gulped down every imaginable form of chemical additive, and vigorous squirming in the middle of an overheated mob produced a sort of benumbed excitement in them, made up of physical contacts that could lead as easily to sex as to violence. Love in the time of sardines. Lucio, Rocco, and Denis were in their natural habitat, determined to become part of that bubbling magma whose ultimate purpose was to achieve a manifold coupling with the first available sardinette they managed to catch.

It was Denis who spied the sardinette. She was fifteen, at the oldest sixteen. She wore a pair of jeans so low and snug on her hips that they were a clear invitation to slip your hand inside. She had a lunar complexion, sky-blue eyes, and a fleshy strawberry for a mouth. Her scent was natural. Incredibly, even her sweat smelled good. And she had a child's voice that drove him wild when she shouted, "My name's Martina," over the booming speakers that throbbed like the veins of Kurt Angle, the professional wrestler.

After giving her a dose of ecstasy that would knock a horse on its ass, Denis pretended to read her palm, pronouncing, seriously: "It seems to me that you have problems with your parents." It was the most obvious thing to say—all kids have problems with their parents. But Martina's eyes had lit up with admiration and, in confirmation of his skills as a seer, she had confided that she had been able to blackmail her father into letting her come to the rave because she had caught him eating Nutella in the garage.

Denis had nodded, in perfect empathy, and after scowling menacingly at some guy who had stepped on his Reeboks, he proffered a pearl of profound wisdom: "The bad thing about parents isn't so much that they're your Mom and Dad, the problem is more that you're their daughter." After that, she let him take her by hand, and she looked up at him with an adoring gaze as they made their way upstream, against the current, finally attaining the exit sign that pointed the way to paradise: the reclinable seats of the Cherokee. To the highly toxic blend of amphetamines he had ingested, he had added one of his father's Viagras, as a little extra insurance. The sardinette was pleased with the results; or, at least, she was until the doors of the Jeep Cherokee swung open and Lucio and Rocco climbed in to join the party. Then the little idiot started yelling that she wanted to go back to join her girlfriends. The she started screaming for her mother. "Make up your mind, little girl—do you want your girlfriends or your mother?" That was Rocco's contribution, in an attempt to downplay the drama. She kept screaming, so Rocco put the Jeep in gear and peeled out. The last thing they wanted was for all that yelling to spoil the big Event. Lucio decided to forget about their little party; he ordered Rocco to pull over and let the girl go. This time, Rocco told him to fuck himself. He pushed harder on the gas, and the

Jeep Cherokee went swerving and jolting down that damned dirt road. Everyone in the Jeep was bouncing in the air like those watermelons you see in the back of the Mexican flatbed ~~~~~~~~~ ~~~~~~~~~~ even though the

was the night they had ~~~~~~~~

When the pair of vehicles finally came to a halt, there were two survivors: the guy driving the cement truck and Lucio, who was still breathing, though it was impossible to tell his arms from his legs. That was how the Carabinieri found him. They hurriedly loaded him onto an ambulance, which had sounded its siren out of a sense of duty more than anything else. They were certain that he'd be dead long before they reached the hospital.

Their pity for the victim didn't last long, though. As they were extracting the corpses of Martina, Rocco, and Denis from the wreckage, the Carabinieri found thirty-five thousand euros in cash, a set of emerald jewelry, a string of pearls, and about thirty rings, including two wedding bands. The dashboard had exploded on impact, spraying projectiles of loot everywhere in the car. The Carabinieri had no need to leap to conclusions; it was more a matter of acknowledging a proven fact.

* * *

The bottle of Sambuca was almost empty. Astrid, the television fortuneteller, looked to her like a Madonna, with the scarf wrapped around her head and the jewelry dangling from her neck and ears. The telephone receiver pressed against her ear was slick with warm sweat. Paola Cavasin had been on hold for forty-five minutes, waiting her turn to talk. But now that she was finally connected to the fortuneteller herself, she couldn't manage to find the words to express the weight pressing down on her heart, the sensation of anguish that even the Sambuca failed to assuage. Also, she was bewildered by the horrible fishtank effect produced by the silent television. They had told her to turn down the sound entirely—to "prevent an annoying feedback effect," is what she thought they'd said. So she would speak into the phone, and then Astrid would answer her over the phone, moving her lips soundlessly, like a giant fish. How could they have a conversation like this? And yet Astrid seemed to have an answer for everything. It was as if she could see the bottle of liqueur hidden under the coffee table through the television screen.

"I know he's cheating on me with those awful women, he doesn't even try to hide it from me anymore. Lucio has figured it out by now."

"Who is Lucio?" asked Astrid, moving her lips to ask the question a full second or two after Paola heard it come through the phone.

"My son," she answered. And she felt like crying when she said it.

"How old is he?" asked the fortuneteller.

Paola couldn't seem to focus. Before she could answer, she always had to wait for Astrid's lips to stop moving.

"Eighteen. I can't take this anymore. What should I do?"

"Paola, now calm down and listen to me carefully. I have something important to tell you."

Paola leaned forward, closer to the television screen.

In the video picture, the fortuneteller selected a card from a tarot deck. The card seemed to worry her quite a bit. She turned it over once, and then turned it over again, the way you wonder how to

could

"I am going to give you this amulet, and it everywhere you go. It is a very powerful amulet, and I am giving it to you because an amulet can only be bestowed as a gift. This amulet is a catalyzer of benign forces. You must keep it on your person at all times, when you hug your son. You must keep it for a week, then I want you to come see me. But take my advice and never let it out of your sight, off of your person . . ."

Clinging desperately to the television, the telephone, and the slender thread of hope, Paola hadn't noticed that her doorbell had been ringing imperiously for several seconds.

Astrid called her name: "Paola?"

The fortuneteller looked out at something or someone on the other side of the video screen. Paola thought that she might be trying to glimpse her front door, but perhaps there was just a director standing next to the television camera. Her next-door neighbor, Elda, had been in the studio audience for "Passaparola" once, and she had explained to Paola that there are lots of people signaling to one another, inside the television.

"Paola, are you still there? Maybe you have to go and answer the door . . ."

"Yes, that's right."

"Well then, for now I'll bid you farewell. Make sure to leave your address with the phone attendant for the amulet, and call me back. Ciao, darling."

Astrid's lips kept on moving, but in the telephone what she heard now was a pre-recorded voice asking her for her name and address, so that they could send her the precious amulet.

"Open up, it's the Carabinieri."

That wasn't the voice from the telephone. Paola put down the receiver, forgetting to provide her address, and tried to get to her feet.

After she finally managed to unhook the security chain, slide back the bolt, and turn first the top key, then the bottom one, the door seemed to swing open on its own. Even a few hours later, she couldn't seem to remember whether or not she had turned the handle, just as she wasn't sure if she'd asked who was at the door. Sure, they had said they were Carabinieri, but that doesn't mean anything. You can say "Carabinieri" and still be an armed criminal. As she was opening the door, she hadn't even thought to look through the peephole. The voice had sounded honest, so she just opened the door. It was a good thing, too, because they really were the Carabinieri. They had all looked at her with a strange expression, then the oldest Carabiniere, a handsome man with salt-and-pepper curly grey hair and a southern accent, had told her something about Lucio. That he'd been in a car crash, but that he wasn't dead, thank God, but then they asked her if they could take a look at his bedroom, in fact, before she knew it, they were searching the whole house, and she could just imagine what her animal of a husband would have to say about that. But if Lucio was hurt and in the hospital, what were they looking for? Giacomo was certain to lose his temper: he'd take it out on her first, because she'd let them in, and after that on Lucio. Lucio—just as the fortuneteller had predicted, had fallen in with bad company.

aged to nail him yet. That was why he was in the situation. Giacomo Zuglio, suspected of money laundering and loan sharking, was only a worried father, while the real criminal was his son, an eighteen-year-old boy who was scheduled to take his high school final exams this year.

The house was expensive, but even he, who was nothing more than an underpaid inspector, understood at a glance that there was money and nothing more. There was none of that history, elegance, taste that you can't even define clearly, but it leaves a bad taste in your mouth when it's not there. It's not so much the furniture itself, it's how the furniture is arranged, or else it's the feeling that certain houses seem to have been there for centuries, and the passage of time has made them elegant and attractive, or, as people say, understated. Zuglio's little villa, which must have been 2,700 square feet with a nice location, had something about it that corresponded more to the people who lived in it than to the house itself. There was too much furniture, when a single nice painting would have been sufficient, sofas upholstered with different types of fabric—

solid pink here, a floral pattern there. It was an unholy mess to look at, in other words, as if the architect who had designed the house had one thing in mind, and then the minute he left, the Zuglio family had set about betraying that vision without even realizing it.

This sequence of musings had lasted no more than a handful of seconds, of course. The inspector was certainly not the kind of person to spend a lot of time thinking about interior decoration. While he unleashed his men to search the various rooms in the house, he asked where the son's room was— Lucio's room. It was no simple matter to get that information, because the poor woman was buzzing from one room to another, like a crazed housefly. She seemed to be somewhat deranged, too. That bottle of Sambuca under the coffee table in the living room probably had something to do with that. It was always useful in his line of work to guess certain things on the spur of the moment, though he wasn't there to investigate the woman. He was there to see if he could recover the bulk of the swag, because if they'd found all that loot in the Cherokee, there would probably be more, much more, in the house, unless the son of the loan shark and the deranged housefly had been crafty enough to hide the plunder somewhere else. He doubted it, though. Young men, at least that kind of young man, assume that they're immune to the rules of the game. And since the young man in question still lived at home, he ignored dresser drawers, armoire, and mattress—the obvious targets of paternal searches—and focused on the wooden baseboard. The main difficulty involved was kneeling down to pry it away from the wall, because he had the back of a fifty-five-year-old policeman who had spent the last thirty years manning road-blocks and checkpoints in the foggy winter weather of the north, or in the driver's seat of an Alfa Romeo squad car. It took him a little longer than ten minutes to find the stash—a hole carved out behind the baseboard in a corner, hidden behind a linen chest. In the cavity, he found jewelry, bundles of cash, and even a pistol with a mother-of-pearl handle. But what made him lean his aching back against the wall was a photograph, a snapshot showing the boy, Lucio Zuglio, in the company of Gi...

"Lucio Zuglio."

"Zuglio?" I exclaimed in surprise. "Is he related to Giacomo Zuglio by any chance?"

"He's his son. Do you know Giacomo?"

"No."

Mele gave me a funny look. "Then why did you ask about him?"

"Just curious. I've heard his name before."

Mele sighed dubiously and then told me about the chain of events that had led to the discovery of the Polaroid in the young man's bedroom. "It was carefully concealed," he explained. "He definitely didn't want it to be found."

"Is he the one?"

Mele took back the photograph and slid it into a folder marked with the coat of arms of the Carabinieri. He was ill at ease. "I can't say. I'm waiting for him to recover a little before questioning him, but he seems too young to fit in with the phrase reported by the witness, Carla Pisani . . ."

"I understand," I broke in.

"In any case, Zan intends to name him as a suspect for murder. No matter what else happens, when they release him from the hospital he's going to spend some time in prison. In the meanwhile, we'll proceed with DNA testing."

I pointed to the folder. "That picture was taken in a restaurant."

"It's not a local restaurant. We're trying to track it down."

I stood up and extended my hand. "Thank you for letting me know about this."

Mele stood up, too. "Is there something you want to tell me?"

"I beg your pardon?"

"You don't really think I believe you just happen to have heard Giacomo Zuglio's name?"

The inspector looked at me with the expression of someone whose job it is to question people and catch them in contradictions or implausible statements. He had seen me make a misstep, and he wasn't going to be placated with a shrug of the shoulders.

"Giovanna mentioned the name," I lied. "Her father had had dealings with Zuglio a little while before his furniture factory burned down."

Mele nodded with a poker face. "As soon as we have news, I'll let you know."

Outside the barracks, I found Beggiolin waiting for me. "Counselor Visentin, are you relieved to learn that your fiancée's murderer is safely in the hands of the law?"

"That strikes me as premature . . ."

"Are you expecting an example to be made of this young man? Will you join the prosecution as a civil plaintiff?" he interrupted me.

"Provided there is actually a trial."

Beggiolin gestured to the cameraman to stop filming.

"What on earth are you saying?" he asked furiously. "I'm here to help pave the way for you, to make sure that little asshole gets sentenced to life without parole, and all you can do is piss and moan about reasonable doubt?"

"Don't you dare speak to me in that tone," I warned him. "And be clear on this: there is no evidence that Lucio Zuglio murdered Giovanna."

"Oh there isn't? How many of our fellow townspeople keep photographs of Giovanna Barovier hidden behind the baseboard in their bedroom and go around attacking women in their homes as a pastime?"

His logic was impeccable, for a local television station. I decided to say nothing, and just walked away.

"He was the one," yelled Beggiolin. "Get used to it. He was sleeping with your fiancée, and then he killed her."

I holed up in my house and disconnected the phone. I was more and more confused. Immediately after the name of Giacomo Zuglio emerges as a potential suspect, the son's name pops up as well. That Giovanna knew him and saw him socially was certain. That photograph provided all the evidence needed. Giovanna's gaze as they sat at the same table in that restaurant was calm and relaxed and affectionate. Was it possible that Lucio really was her lover and her murderer? I tried to turn the matter over and over again in my mind in order to figure out what it all meant. It was baffling and I finally gave up. As I walked back and forth in the room I happened to look over at Giovanna's digital camera, the one I'd found at Prunella's house. I switched it on and started toggling through the images contained in the camera's memory. Our Paris trip, a mountain hike, a dinner party at a friend's house . . . I looked at an image of myself smiling. I wondered if I'd ever be able to smile again. As I punched buttons more or less at random, I discovered that the memory also held a sixty-second video.

Nowadays, digital technology was capable of transforming a little hand-held still camera into a tiny video camera.

Suddenly I saw Giovanna. She was barefoot, wearing a negligée. From the tiny speaker I heard her voice. "Come on, cut it out," she was saying, in a voice that was both playful and charged with sensuality.

"Come on, stop it," she repeated, shutting a door in the camera's face. I rewound the video. I watched it again, then for a third and a fourth time. Then I slumped down on the sofa.

Giovanna was talking to her killer. She was flirting with him, playing with him before taking him to bed, dressed in a department-store negligée. I was all too familiar with the way she was talking, the way she was looking into and away from the camera. This was the prelude to love, desire, and pleasure. I mastered my feelings. I pulled out my laptop computer, plugged in the jack, and uploaded the video. Giovanna appeared on the twelve-inch screen. I watched the video over and over again until the most obvious thing about it finally occurred to me. This hadn't been shot in her house. I zoomed in on the details of the furniture. Inexpensive, but denoting a certain taste. It was all furniture from the turn of the twentieth century; farmhouse furniture that had been cleaned and restored. I had never been in that house, of that I was certain. "Find the house, and you'll find the murderer," I thought to myself as I zoomed in on Giovanna's face. I wanted to observe her hairstyle closely to figure out exactly when the video had been shot. It had to have been recently. No more than three months old. Until then, she'd worn her hair long, with bangs.

What I should have done was go straight to Mele and turn over the video to him, but it would have become part of the investigator's files. Zan would watch it. And if the murderer was ever caught and put on trial, the court would be able to watch it. Perhaps the whole town would see it, if Beggiolin managed to lay his hands on it. I didn't want the whole town

to think of Giovanna as a whore. Even if that's how I thought
of her now. Until that moment, I had continued to love her and
to justify her. The phrase that Carla had related to me had mis-
led me until then. In the video, she certainly gave no impression of having been forced to become the slut of the man who
had ruined her life. She looked much more like a woman
cheating on her future husband with a man she liked very
much. She had even let him film her, and she had kept the
video. I wondered how many times she had played it back for
herself. I hoped there weren't any other videos. Giovanna had
been murdered, and she deserved justice, no matter what had
happened. Those images would remain burned into my memory for the rest of my life. I would never be able to remember
anything else about Giovanna. If I ever wanted to be free of
her smiling phantom in a negligée I would have to find her
murderer. Only by ensuring that he had been punished could
I hope to recover the modicum of serenity that I would need
to rebuild my life.

My first impulse was to check to see if the house in the
video was Zuglio's, but the rest of the Antenna N/E news was
enough to rule that out. At the end of a report on the capers of
the home invasion gang, tying them without a second thought
to Giovanna's murder, Beggiolin announced an interview with
Giacomo Zuglio.

The interview was done in the living room of the Zuglio
home, as Beggiolin announced in the introduction. From the
very first shot I could tell this wasn't the house in the video.

"Signore Zuglio, what does it mean to a father to discover
that his son is a criminal?" asked the television reporter in a
voice filled with empathy.

"A knife in the heart . . . a sense of failure," replied the former bank officer. "You think you've taught your son certain
values, and instead you find . . ."

He couldn't finish the sentence, overwhelmed as he was by

his feelings. Beggiolin didn't push him, but the camera focused relentlessly on the hands that covered the man's face.

"Will you stand by his side, in this moment of family tragedy?" the reporter asked after a suitable pause.

Giacomo Zuglio put down his hands and looked steadily into the lens. "From this moment on, Lucio has ceased to be my son."

You could hear a woman's despairing wail. The television camera swung to another part of the room, and I saw a woman crumpled in an armchair, clutching her sides in grief and pain. Beggiolin hastily introduced her.

"Giacomo Zuglio's wife and the boy's mother, Paola," he whispered softly into the microphone, careful not to disturb the audio of her sobs.

I switched off the television set. After that news item, no one in town would have any doubts about Lucio Zuglio's guilt. At least not until the DNA results came back.

Alvise and Carla were so insistent that I finally had to give in and agree to meet them. My father called me that morning. He had heard about Lucio's arrest and had managed to move his depature forward. He would be back in two days.

"The boy has nothing to do with this," Alvise said immediately, as he poured himself a glass of red wine.

"How can you be so sure?"

"Because I know it, and the DNA test will prove me right," he answered resentfully. "We need to keep investigating the father."

"What have you found out?" Carla asked.

"I'm looking into the corporate structure. I think I'll have something solid by the end of the week," I replied, doing my best to sound convincing.

"There was another fish kill," Carla said in a worried voice. "I ran new tests, and that soil is increasingly toxic."

"Let's hope they move the toxic waste soon."

Carla sighed gloomily. "The toxic substances have leached into the soil. We need a serious clean-up, or there could be serious risk for the local population."

"The pollutants could get into the groundwater," Alvise warned.

I looked at them both. Clearly they had talked things over at length and they had come to a few decisions.

"What are you planning to do?" I asked.

"Unless we make some serious progress in the next few days, we have to report the existence of the waste dump to the Carabinieri," Carla answered.

"Let's wait just one more week," I suggested. "Let's see what the investigators turn up on Lucio Zuglio and what information I manage to find about the Eco T.D.W."

Carla and Alvise agreed. Before leaving, I reached into my pocket and pulled out a print I had made from the video. Of course, you couldn't see Giovanna. Instead there was a kitchen cupboard, the edge of a table, two chairs and, in the background, a window.

I showed it to Carla. "Have you ever seen this room?"

"No," she answered, confidently. "Whose house is it?"

"I don't know. But I found this photograph among Giovanna's papers."

At last my father came back from Romania. He called me after landing in Verona, and when he entered the law offices, I was there waiting for him.

"Prunella called me," he reported as he wrapped me in a hug. "She's asking me to represent her as civil plaintiff in the criminal case against Lucio Zuglio."

"Shouldn't we wait for the findings of the DNA test?"

"No. Always remember, if you are representing the civil plaintiff you have to support openly everything the criminal investigators do from the very outset. It's an old trick; it helps to make the court your ally."

"Do you think he's guilty?"

He smiled. "I'm astonished you would ask me such a thing. You know how I feel about the presumption of innocence."

"You have a point," I admitted. I stood up and walked over to the window. A light drizzle had been falling relentlessly since morning. The wet stone façades of the buildings in the center of town were glistening in the light of the streetlamps. "I have to give you some bad news," I said suddenly.

Papa looked up from a file that his secretary had left for him on his desk. "How bad?" he asked, knitting the fingers of his hands together.

I told him about the secret waste dump, and about Zuglio and Trevisan. I only left out the fact that Alvise had come back. As long as he remained in hiding, it seemed reasonable to keep his secret. Papa turned pale once he began to grasp how serious matters had become.

"Trevisan has abused my trust," he commented in horror. "I helped him in the name of our old friendship."

"What do you plan to do?"

"I need some time, and I especially need to keep this quiet," he replied. "You can assure Carla Pisani that the soil will be cleaned up, at Foundation expense, as soon as is humanly possible."

"Will you arrange to report Zuglio and the Romanian to the police?"

My father looked straight at me. "When I talked about keeping this quiet, that's what I meant. An investigation into the actions of these scoundrels could easily uncover the role played by the Eco T.D.W. and the fact that it belongs to the cartel of corporations linked to the Foundation."

"I don't understand. These are serious crimes."

"Not so very serious. It's a small-time fraud, and in Italy, trafficking in toxic wastes is punished with a ridiculously light sentence."

"I disagree," I replied. "Most important, I'm quite sure I can't make Carla keep quiet about this."

"If this story becomes public the damage to the image of the Foundation will be irreparable," he explained in a heartfelt tone. "A scandal would become a formidable weapon in the hands of our competitors. The Foundation is going through a delicate transition. As I've told you, we are transferring all our operations to Romania." He stood up and walked over to me. "I vouched for Trevisan. I would be the first to pay for that mistake, and I don't deserve it."

"I'll do what I can," I promised.

I left the law offices baffled and disappointed. I could understand that Papa was in a delicate situation, but I would have liked to see a different attitude, a little less eager to engage in a cover-up.

I still had a few days to decide what to do. I had no intention of continuing to keep the truth from Carla but, for the moment, that was still the simplest way to manage the situation.

The newspapers and Antenna N/E played up the story of Prunella's decision to become a civil plaintiff. "We have no prejudices against Lucio Zuglio. We are merely emphasizing Signora Barovier's determination to obtain justice for her daughter Giovanna," my father had declared with as much cunning as diplomacy.

That same day, a blood sample was taken from Lucio Zuglio, who was still in the hospital, in serious condition. The public defender had raised no objections, nor had the defendant. I doubted that proper procedures had been followed, but it was none of my business, and more than anything else, I wanted to find out the test results.

It was a bitter surprise to learn that it would be impossible to do any DNA testing because of the deterioration of the one sample capable of providing scientific identification of the murderer. As my father had confided to me, Professor Marizza had assured him that he would do everything within his power to ensure that the seminal fluid could not be used as evidence against me. But I felt certain that he would pull back once I had been ruled out as a suspect in the days immediately following. In a press conference, Prosecutor Zan stated that the definitive piece of evidence to prove Lucio Zuglio's guilt had been lost, but that the evidence gathered in the course of the investigation was more than sufficient to warrant an indictment. The defense attorney had nothing to say, and he did nothing in judicial terms. I had worked with him on other cases, and I knew that he was far from incompetent. Evidently, he had decided not to turn the entire town and the courtroom community—first and foremost among them my father—against himself. Beggiolin continued his campaign relentlessly. Every day he aired a new report that dug Lucio Zuglio's grave a little deeper. One thing was certain—whoever the murderer was, if there was no DNA evidence he had a much better chance of getting away with his crime.

Once again, I found myself sitting in front of my computer, analyzing every detail of the video. It had become an obsession. I couldn't keep myself from going back to stare at Giovanna. I was behaving irrationally, and I was masking it behind the need to gather all potential evidence that could help me identify where the video had been shot. I found myself staring into Giovanna's eyes. And she wasn't looking at me. That woman was supposed to be mine, all mine, but instead I was forced to share her with another man. In the end, those were the thoughts crowding into my mind. That night I was stuck on her negligée. I had blown up the hem until it was just a shapeless blob. Then someone rang my doorbell. It was a little past two in the morning. I remembered that I had heard the church bell strike two just ten minutes before. I wondered if it was Mele. Maybe Lucio Zuglio had confessed or had died. Instead, I opened the door to Alvise.

"I have to talk to you," he announced in a brusque tone of voice.

He had wine on his breath, but he wasn't drunk. He must have gulped down a glass before leaving Carla's apartment and stepping out in the chilly night air. I ushered him into the living room.

"I'm worried about Lucio," he said. "I have a hunch that they're trying to frame him, just like they framed me."

"Why are you so concerned about what happens to that young man?"

"Because he's my son."

"His mother, Paola, was my secretary. And my lover. The night the factory burned down I was with her," Alvise explained to me, once I had recovered from my astonishment.

"Why didn't you say that when they arrested you?" I asked in genuine surprise.

He smiled at me bitterly. "To keep her from looking like a slut to the whole town, I provided a false alibi. When they uncovered it, it was too late to retract. They would never have believed me."

"Did she already know she was pregnant?"

"No. She found out later. Don Piero brought me the news. He also told me that Giacomo Zuglio was willing to marry her immediately if I promised to keep matters secret."

"Did they know each other?"

"Paola had to go to the bank frequently for business, and he was courting her. She had always turned him down, but in the end Zuglio got what he wanted anyway."

I thought back to the photograph of Giovanna and Lucio in the restaurant.

"How did Giovanna find out that she had a brother?"

"I don't know that. She only told me that she'd found out and that she'd told Lucio about it, too."

"So they couldn't have been lovers," I thought aloud.

"And Lucio is innocent. What can we do to help him?" he said.

"Tell them everything. Are you willing?"

The next day, even though it was a Sunday, I went to talk with Mele. The officer on duty told me he was off duty, and I had to insist repeatedly before he would call him. He came down a few minutes later. Like the other non-commissioned officers he lived in an apartment building constructed twenty years earlier inside the perimeter of the barracks compound. He was in civilian clothing and his hands were covered with flour.

"I was making pasta dough," he explained.

"I have a witness who can clear Lucio Zuglio as a suspect in Giovanna's murder."

"Tell him to come to the office tomorrow morning."

"I would prefer to organize a meeting with Zan, the defense lawyer, and the civil plaintiff."

"A slight deviation from protocol" he commented sarcastically. "And your father is in agreement?"

"I haven't told him yet."

He gave me a questioning look. "He represents the civil plaintiff," he reminded me.

"Oh, I'm well aware of that. This is a delicate matter, I'd like to take care of it quickly and quietly."

"And who is this witness?" he asked acidly. "One of the usual bigwigs that have to be treated with kid gloves, otherwise they might get their feelings hurt?"

"No. He's nobody, just a loser."

He reached out for the telephone. "Let's see what Zan has to say." The conversation lasted a couple of minutes. "This evening, at seven," he said. With a smile, he added, "You ruined the prosecutor's Sunday."

I returned home and reported the latest developments to Alvise, who had just stepped out of the shower wrapped in my bathrobe. It had been a gift from Giovanna. I was certainly not going to bother washing it after he left. It would go straight into the garbage. Barovier had slept in the guest bedroom. I insisted that he stay at my house; if he went back to Carla's, it would only deepen her involvement in this mess. I watched him as he read the paper. He wore a pair of unfashionable old eyeglasses. I wasn't sure that he was fully aware of what awaited him. And as I later had occasion to learn, neither was I. A law degree and a few small cases aren't enough to make someone a good lawyer. It takes experience.

We arrived at the barracks a few minutes after the time appointed by Zan. The others were already there, sitting in the inspector's office. When Alvise entered the room, my father was the only one who recognized him.

"Alvise," he exclaimed in surprise.

Alvise wouldn't deign to look at him, and sat down across from the prosecutor. My father gave me a stern glance of reproof. He must have been furious that he hadn't been told the identity of the witness. After the initial formalities had been gotten out of the way, Barovier told his version of Lucio's story. I had advised him to leave out all the other issues. Especially not to say anything about Giovanna's campaign to clear his name. It was still too early.

Then it was my turn to wrap up. "Of course, Signore Barovier is ready and willing to have a DNA test to prove his paternity."

Zan reacted in an agitated manner. His prosecution theory had crumbled before his eyes. The investigation into the murder of Giovanna Barovier was by no means over. "This means nothing," he blurted out in a hysterical voice. "There's no evidence that Giovanna Barovier actually told Zuglio that they were close relatives. Moreover, you are an ex-convict . . ."

"Let it go, Zan," my father interrupted him. "The theory you're setting forth wouldn't convince a grand jury, much less a criminal court."

"I request that my client be released and the case against him dropped," the court-appointed defense counsel timidly ventured in a timid voice.

"Present an official request," snarled the prosecutor. "And I won't even give it my consideration until we receive the test results."

My father cleared his throat to attract attention. "Zan, I'd like you to ask the witness about his movements the night of the murder."

"Do you think I killed her?" Alvise demanded furiously.

"I don't think anything," my father replied with chilly formality. "All I know is that you came back to town after fifteen years, at the very moment when your daughter was being murdered. It strikes me that the circumstance deserves some exploration."

"Well?" the prosecutor prompted Alvise.

Barovier gave me a worried look. He had had some ugly experiences that had begun in a similar setting, and he was afraid of saying the wrong thing.

I decided to intervene. "I would like to point out, and I shouldn't have to remind those present, that Giovanna had sexual intercourse before being murdered . . ."

"Before," Zan pointed out. "He could certainly have arrived at his daughter's house after her lover left."

"And do we think Giovanna would welcome the father she hadn't seen in fifteen years, nude, in a bathtub?"

The prosecutor didn't know how to respond to that point. He looked at my father, in hope of a suggestion.

"I wonder if you could ask the witness where and why he remained hidden until this evening," said Papa. "I don't remember seeing him anywhere around his daughter's coffin during the funeral, nor as far as I am aware did he make himself available to the investigating authorities."

"Why and where are my own business," Alvise replied with exasperation. "If you want to accuse me of a crime, be my guests. Otherwise, I've said what I have to say, and you've taken careful note."

"You are a witness," Zan shot back. "You are required to answer."

Barovier shook his head and lapsed into an obstinate silence.

I was obliged to intervene to help him out. "Signore Barovier came back to Italy to attend his daughter Giovanna's wedding, and she was planning to offer him a place to stay," I lied confidently. "The news of the murder threw him into a serious fit of depression, and he took shelter in a ruined country house near town. Then he turned to me, as Giovanna's former fiancé, and I immediately contacted Inspector Mele."

My father rose to his feet. "The civil plaintiff acknowledges the witness's testimony."

Zan did the same. Alvise signed his statement and left the room without another word. Lucio was now in no danger of being tried for Giovanna's murder, but Alvise had been subjected to a humiliating interrogation.

"Bastards," he hissed once we were back in the car. "And your father is the worst of the lot. He had the gall to accuse me of killing Giovanna."

"He was pretty tough, but the lawyer for the civil plaintiff has no alternative. I'm the one who owes you an apology. I should have known that the questioning would be ugly. I could have spared you that hail of questions."

A bitter smile creased his face like a wound. "You're a rank beginner," he declared. But he added immediately: "Still, I'd choose you as a defense lawyer over your father."

I drove him to a motel out on the provincial highway. "I can't afford it," he said.

"Don't worry about it. I've already talked to the proprietor. Tomorrow I'll go pick up your belongings from Carla's apartment."

Alvise stepped out of the car and started walking toward the reception desk. He was staggering like a punchdrunk boxer who's just lost yet another match.

I wanted to go back home, turn on the computer, and watch that video over and over again. I hadn't shot up my daily dose of that beautiful woman in a negligée saying, "Come on, cut it out." Instead, I had to face my father. Giovanna would have to wait for me a little longer.

He was wearing an English-style dressing gown and he had a scarf wrapped around his neck. The scarf matched his slippers. He didn't say a word to me when I walked into the living room. He had a book in his hands, but I felt certain that he hadn't been able to read a single line while he was waiting for me to arrive.

He rose from the armchair and pointed his index finger at me. "You made me look like a fool. You should have told me it was Alvise."

"Is that why you savaged him the way you did?"

"He was capable of burning a whole family in their sleep to cash in on an insurance policy. Forgive me if I have a few suspicions about him."

"Well, now everything's all cleared up."

"You can't think that I believed his fairytale about being invited to the wedding. Prunella would never have allowed that to happen, as she just confirmed over the phone."

"Get over it. There's nothing more to it."

"No. There's still one thing: I want to know why he came back."

"Then why don't you ask him yourself?"

"Whose side are you on?"

"Whose side are *you* on, Papa?! If it's true that the night the furniture factory burned down Alvise was with Paola, then it means he's innocent. That possibility doesn't seem to bother you in the slightest."

"He's guilty as sin. And Paola is a hopeless alcoholic. For a drop of whiskey, she'd say anything you tell her to say."

"How do you know that? Do you know the Zuglio family?"

"I gathered a little information about them in connection with that matter of the toxic waste dump. By the way, have you spoken with Carla Pisani?"

"Not yet."

"Why not?" he insisted.

"I haven't come up with a convincing lie to palm off on her yet," I answered with exasperation.

As I was leaving, I ran into the cook. She was waiting for me at the door, and she handed me a tray covered with a napkin. "A little something for your sweet tooth," she whispered in an affectionate tone. I muttered a hasty thank-you and left the house.

In the car, I unwrapped the napkin and discovered that it was a tray of fried cream squares. A true delicacy of Venetian cuisine. My mother had taught her how to make them. I popped a section into my mouth and put the car in gear. I ate the rest in front of the computer. Giovanna wasn't crazy about sweets, as I reminded her image under my breath, as I painstakingly enlarged a mirror. In that mirror it was just possible to glimpse a blurry shadow. That was him. Her lover. Her murderer.

For Beggiolin, losing Lucio as Giovanna's murderer wasn't a serious setback. On the contrary. The news of Alvise Barovier's mysterious arrival in town and the unexpected revelation that he was the boy's real father only opened the door to a series of gripping reports. He managed to find Alvise's motel and got an interview with him. The rapid-fire succession of innuendo-laden questions tripped Alvise up repeatedly. And the crowning blow was a piece on the old episode of arson. Man-in-the-street interviews done around town presented a harsh view of Barovier. The relatives of the victims of the fire suggested he ought to go back to Argentina. But Beggiolin's real victim was Paola. Giacomo Zuglio, once the story became public knowledge, stayed out of sight, even though Beggiolin had portrayed him as a man who had been capable of a gesture of great humanity and generosity, by marrying a woman who was about to bear the child of a convicted felon. The television reporter managed to get inside her house and pepper the poor alcoholic woman with questions. She managed to stammer out insults against her husband, Giacomo, who spent his time flirting and sleeping with those wild women. Then she begged for lenient treatment for Lucio. It broke my heart. Astrid, the town fortuneteller, also made her appearance in the report. Beggiolin hadn't even had to walk across the street to interview her: she did her broadcast from the same building. Of course, Astrid claimed to have foreseen everything that happened, and even managed to find recordings of a few of Paola's calls to her show. No one showed the slightest pity for the poor woman. No one in town, certainly, where nobody talked about anything else, and where every television set was tuned to Antenna N/E. Giovanna's murder had become the setting for a story abounding in savory plot twists, turns, and surprises. There was a steadily diminishing interest in the effort to identify the guilty party.

Alvise came to see me a couple of days later.

"I walked from one end of the town to the other," he said. "With my head held high. And when anyone stopped to stare at me, I stopped and asked them what the fuck they were looking at. Do you think that one person had the courage to answer me?"

I knew the answer to that question and I did nothing more than look at him in an understanding manner. He was even sadder and more hopeless than before. "I've come to ask you for help," he announced, taking a seat on the sofa.

"If there's anything I can do, I'm glad to."

"I want to do something to help Paola and Lucio, but I have no money, and I certainly can't look for a job here in town," he explained. "I'm going to have to go back to Argentina, but I don't want to leave without finding out who killed Giovanna. But you could help them."

"What can I do for them? And frankly, you know, they're strangers to me."

He seized me by the hand. "You have money and you're a lawyer. Paola needs to go somewhere far away from that house and dry out. And Lucio needs a real lawyer. You wouldn't want to leave him in the hands of that idiot . . ."

I wriggled my hand out of his grip. "How is Lucio?" I asked.

"He's pretty beat up, but the doctors say he'll recover," he answered. Then he looked at me.

"I went to see him every day. At first he refused to talk to me. I didn't push it, until finally today I found the courage to tell him about when I was in prison and couldn't see Giovanna because Prunella kept her from coming to visit me. He asked me about prison, and I told him that it's impossible to survive if there's no one on the outside waiting for you."

"What do you expect from me?" I cried, getting to my feet. "For fifteen years, you took no interest in either of them. But now you want someone else to take care of them, in your place, while you head back to Argentina. Pretty easy on you."

"Lucio is so young," he begged me. "He has only lived a tiny part of his life, a miserable part. But he can put that all behind him now. He has a right to a future."

"I already said it, that's not my job."

He stood up and put on his heavy jacket. "It's too bad Giovanna is dead," he whispered as he slipped the oversized buttons into the buttonholes. "She would have helped them."

I was surprised to see how many people attended the requiem mass commemorating the thirtieth day since Giovanna's death. Alvise was the last to arrive and the first to leave the church, followed by Prunella's baleful glare. When I walked over to speak to her, she made a big show of avoiding my embrace. "Get away from me!" she hissed at me, loud enough to attract attention. "It's your fault that everyone is talking about us."

I was about to deliver a sharp answer, but Carla took my arm and accompanied me out of the church.

"Look what I found," she said. She pulled a handful of paper strips out of her purse and put them in my hand.

"What are they?"

"It's what's left of papers that were fed through a shredder. It's all that's left of the documentation concerning the Eco T.D.W. that was archived at the local health board," she replied. "They're cleaning house while we sit on our asses. I'm sick of doing nothing. I'm going to report them before it's too late."

"No. Come to my house. I have to talk to you."

I had decided to level with her. She didn't deserve to be lied to. When I finished telling her about my father's plan, she smoked in silence for a while.

"You can't ask me to become an accomplice to these people," she said, puffing out a cloud of cigarette smoke.

"That's not exactly what I'm asking you, and after all, the soil will be cleaned up, and the companies will move to Romania."

She shook her head in disappointment. "And then everything will be fine, right?"

"Exactly."

"Open your eyes, Francesco. They're going to transform the clean-up into a way of making money. They'll get funds from the regional government. Trevisan will probably get the contract for the job. And have you really not grasped why all these companies are moving to China or Romania? It's not just so they can pay their workers lower wages. It's also because there they can pollute all they want without regulation. In those countries, there are no laws protecting the environment, and they won't even be obliged to make use of illegal waste management services anymore. People like Zuglio and Constantin will continue dealing in toxic waste for those who remain behind. Haven't you ever heard the expression 'eco-mafia'?"

"Sure. But that's not what's happening here."

Carla wrinkled her face in a grimace of disgust. "You're so afraid that your father might be in trouble with the law that you can't see the way things really are. When he went into business with Trevisan, he became an accomplice to fraud."

"That's a serious accusation."

"Ferrari destroyed the documentation that was in the local health board files because someone had warned him that the jig was up. It was certainly Trevisan, after his conversation with your father."

"Papa is legal counsel to the Eco T.D.W.," I tried to explain, though only half-heartedly. "In this case, he was acting in his own interest and in the interest of his client. And attorney-client privilege prevented him from talking to anyone about it. Now, what Trevisan chooses to do . . ."

Carla grabbed her purse and her down jacket and headed for the door. "I don't want to sit here listening to this crap anymore."

I grabbed her arm. "Let's try to work out a solution."

"What solution? You're so eager to make your father happy that you've even forgotten that Giovanna may well have been murdered because she uncovered the fraud."

I certainly hadn't forgotten, but I didn't think that it was plausible. I made a decision. "Come with me, I have something to show you."

Carla refused to watch the video for a third time. She turned her back to the screen and lit a cigarette. "Why did you show me that?"

"So that you can understand that this was a crime of passion. Giovanna was the victim in a complicated sexual relationship. Does she strike you as the slut of the man who ruined her life?"

She turned and stared at me. "Maybe not. But Giovanna had stumbled on a toxic waste ring, and I want to find out everything there is to know. Murder and fraud may very well be linked here."

"If you report this to the Carabinieri, you'll ruin a good person's life."

"I don't intend to go to the police immediately."

"Why not?"

"I told you: I want to find out everything there is to know," she replied. "By now Trevisan and his accomplices know that the toxic waste dump has been uncovered, and now they'll have to move the waste somewhere else. I intend to find out where. Then I'll turn them in."

She opened the door and then turned back to speak:

"Don't tell your father about this," she warned me. "Those people wouldn't hesitate to kill me."

* * *

"My mother did her best to toughen me up through a series of educational dinners. When I was just eleven, she forced me to eat meals while trying to enjoy conversations with middle-aged strangers. What a cruel thing to do. Some of the boys my age, in a bid to escape that sort of torture, allowed themselves to be shipped off to boarding schools, in Switzerland, of course, and then they enlisted in the army, choosing the special forces: the San Marco battalion of the Italian marines or the Folgore brigade of paratroopers. When they were discharged, they had been spiritually strengthened, and then they usually married a second cousin, the kind of woman who plays bridge with the curtains drawn because daylight gives her a migraine headache. Do you play bridge, doctor?"

Moroncini said nothing. He did no more, as usual, than to scrawl something incomprehensible in his Moleskine.

This was the twelfth session. Selvaggia had decided to intensify the therapy because so far she had not seen any results. Selvaggia was in a hurry. She was no longer going to tolerate Filippo's laziness, and she was certainly not happy about all the hours he spent in the wine cellar, where Filippo devoted more and more of his time to perfecting his new Sauvignon, and in his studio, where that horrendous sculpture stood on a table, even though as far as she was concerned it had been finished long ago.

For his part, Moroncini had canceled his appointments with a couple of patients to make room for Filippo. It was impossible to say no to the Contessa, Filippo was certainly right about that.

Knowing perfectly well that the doctor would never answer him, Filippo went on:

"I don't like closed curtains. They make me think of secrets to be kept, conspiracies to be concealed. They make me think of my mother."

"Are you saying that you hate her?"

"What a ridiculous question. Does a prisoner hate his guards? Of course he does, but at the same time he depends on them. Especially if he hasn't figured out an escape plan yet."

"Then your attempted suicide two years ago was an unsuccessful escape plan?"

"Try to be a little less simplistic, doctor. That's not what my mother pays you for. Believe it or not, I did it for love. And I was wrong, of course. My mother had warned me. You see? I always come back to her. Sooner or later, I'll have to kill her . . ."

Filippo twisted around to enjoy the psychiatrist's reaction; obviously, though, he remained expressionless.

So Filippo sat up on the couch and smiled at his doctor:

"Do you want to know why I hate my mother so much? Do you really want to know the truth?"

Moroncini continued to look at him with a neutral expression. He was all too experienced with this sort of trick from his patients.

Filippo persisted. He leaned forward in a conspiratorial manner and hissed:

"My mother is a murderer."

Filippo Calchi Renier had left his office half an hour ago. Moroncini had no more patients scheduled for that day. He was done going through the notes for his latest book, a short work on the troubled youth of the families of the Northeast. Once he had brought a monkish order to his brier-root desktop, he dialed the number of the Contessa's cellphone. Selvaggia answered on the third ring.

"I am very worried about Filippo."

Selvaggia was sitting next to Professor Moroncini in the back seat of her Mercedes. The Romanian chauffeur had been ordered to drive slowly along seldom-used country roads. They had both agreed not to meet at Villa Selvaggia, lest Filippo happen to see them; as for Moroncini's office, the Contessa was reluctant to allow rumors to spread about her mental health. In this, she was still a farmer's daughter.

"How are the sessions proceeding?" asked Selvaggia, nodding slightly toward the psychiatrist.

"Rather well, I'd say," Moroncini replied laconically.

"It doesn't seem like it. He's become so . . . embarrassing."

"That's a phase of the therapy. They learn to express their resentments."

"You're the expert," commented Selvaggia with a hint of skepticism.

"The other day, for example, he told me that he wants to kill you."

"And you call that progress?"

"Don't you want to know why he hates you so much?"

"That's why I pay you, isn't it? So you'll violate the bond of client-doctor privilege."

"Certainly, but I believe that information of this nature demands a considerable modification of our initial agreement."

"That depends on the nature of the information . . ."

Moroncini paused. It was a long pause. Pauses were one of his specialties.

"Well?" Selvaggia insisted.

"Filippo is convinced that you haven't been entirely truthful about the murder of Giovanna Barovier . . ."

"Filippo is spouting nonsense as usual!"

"That may well be, but in his state of psychological distress, he might decide to talk to the Carabinieri . . ."

Selvaggia took off the dark glasses that she wore even on the cloudiest days. She turned a savage gaze on Moroncini. That gaze was truly terrifying, and it was one of *her* specialties.

"Your information," she informed him, "is of no value. Filippo's undependability is already well known to the investigators. Whatever statement he may choose to make will never undercut my version of events. In part because I have never stated anything but the truth. I'm very sorry to have to tell you this."

Moroncini shrugged in a sign of surrender.

But Selvaggia hadn't finished: "Unless . . ."

The psychiatrist looked at her with interest.

"Unless you are willing to help me have Filippo declared incompetent. A detailed psychiatric report might help to get a court order blocking him from the family business. In exchange, I could provide you with some very interesting and very private information about the new investments that the Foundation is undertaking in Romania."

"To have him declared incompetent, we would have to demonstrate a complete inability to understand or to express intention. It would be disastrous for Filippo . . ."

"Oh, Filippo hates business anyway. He can't take the pressure of responsibility. It would be a relief for him, trust me."

"And it would mean that you would have unlimited control of the entire Calchi Renier estate," Moroncini insinuated.

"Write that report, Professor. In exchange, Counselor Visentin will provide you with a list of companies that will double their capital within a year. Buy a nice bundle of shares immediately, and I assure you that you'll be able to devote yourself to poetry for the rest of your life."

Moroncini smiled. "Not poetry. Race cars."

* * *

The sun had just set. The darkness had suddenly taken over the house, making it even gloomier and more silent. I felt the need to get out, to fill my lungs with bracing cold air. After a short walk, I stepped into a pastry shop that served the best hot chocolate with whipped cream in town. My father had been a regular client for years, and I was served with obsequious alacrity.

It had been four days since my last meeting with Carla. I hadn't heard from her since then, and I hadn't called her either. When she had asked me not to mention her to my father, lest I endanger her life, it was as if she had cracked a whip in my face. When my cell phone rang and I saw her name on the caller ID, I wasn't sure whether or not to answer. When it rang for the fifth time, I looked up and saw that everyone in the shop was looking at me. They knew who I was and now they were wondering what mysterious reason I could have for staring at my cell phone without answering. I punched the green button.

"Three trucks have pulled up; they're loading the drums," she alerted me.

"So they've decided to clean house," I commented in a low voice.

"I think you need to come see this. The view is quite interesting."

"Interesting how?"

"Come here, and on the double," she said, then hung up.

Carla was right. By the light of the powerful spotlights illuminating the ground, it was possible to see quite clearly, through the binoculars, the faces of a number of people.

"Which one is Zuglio?" Carla asked.

"He's the short guy in the beige overcoat; the one who's talking with Trevisan and Constantin."

"Do you know the other ones?"

"I've seen two of them before, here at the dump," I answered. "But I've never seen the other three."

The five thugs worked busily and with precision. Drums and jerry cans were unearthed and loaded onto the trucks. The dogs, excited at the activity, barked continuously. Carla mounted a powerful telephoto lens on her camera body and began shooting.

"I've spent all my savings," she explained, as she adjusted the focus. "I need to ask you a favor," she added, after a short pause. "I need to borrow your car. I would have some problems trying to follow the trucks on my bicycle."

I looked down at Constantin, who had lit yet another cigarette. As he talked, he continually looked around. "I won't let you go on your own."

She lowered the camera and stared at me. "Are you sure? You might get in over your head . . ."

"Stop treating me like a child," I hissed at her.

She gave me a crafty smile.

The trucks lined up, ready to pull out. Constantin, Trevisan, and Zuglio climbed into their repective automobiles and drove off toward town.

"Now it's our turn," I muttered, hoping that I wasn't about to get myself into a world of trouble.

On the Mestre viaduct, the trucks blended in with the other heavy vehicles moving past slowly, under the alert gaze of the highway police. Then they merged onto the highway. Around Bologna we were already certain that they were heading south. They stopped for fuel, and the drivers took advantage of the opportunity to grab a sandwich. And Carla took advantage of the opportunity to take some nice photographs of them and of the license plates of their trucks.

The drivers never went faster than fifty miles per hour. They didn't want to run the risk of being pulled over. Something as simple as a speeding ticket could arouse the curiosity of the police. We followed them, hanging back at least two hundred yards.

"Giovanna wasn't honest with the two of us," Carla said, breaking a silence that had gone on for a good long while.

"I'd have to agree that she wasn't."

"She used me. I was just a pawn in her plan," she added, with resentment in her voice.

"She used everyone. Even herself. And in the end she paid, with her life."

"But we loved her. I was her best friend, you were her fiancé. She shouldn't have treated us this way."

"I try not to judge her. She meant to tell me everything, and that's enough for me."

"Even after seeing that video?"

"Yes. It's just that now I feel a little more detached," I replied, hestitating as I hunted for the right words. "It's hard to explain. Giovanna seems more and more like a ghost imprisoned by a spell, who needs for her murderer to be punished before it can find peace."

"And before it can finally free you to live your own life," she added, sympathetically.

Silence returned. Carla fell asleep. Every so often I turned to look at her, thinking how different from Giovanna she was. I woke her when, shortly after dawn, the trucks left the provincial highway and drove deep into the countryside around Nola. Across the fields, plumes of smoke arose from numerous bonfires.

"The land of fires. The color of the smoke indicates the nature of the filth they are burning," Carla began explaining, as she pointed in various directions. "Black: plastic wastes. Red: phosphorous substances. And the smoke down there is light blue because of the concentration of chromium."

"How is this possible, in broad daylight?" I asked indignantly.

Carla snickered. "Here the Camorra's in charge. Now you know what sort of people Trevisan and Zuglio do business with."

We drove along an irrigation canal; beyond it rose billows of dense, acrid smoke.

"You see, they use bales of rags soaked in solvents or halogen compounds as a base for the fires," she went on explaining. "They pretend they're getting rid of rags, and instead they're getting rid of toxic waste at a cut rate."

We drove off and in the distance we glimpsed a farm, with water buffaloes grazing lazily. "Mozzarella with dioxin," she said with bitter irony. "Here the people get sick and die. Liver cancer, leukemia."

As we were talking, the trucks came to a halt and, after a while, a couple of cars joined them. Through the binoculars I saw a handshake between the drivers and the new arrivals. Carla took a series of photographs, and then she squeezed my arm, hard.

"Let's go, Francesco. I'm afraid."

At last, I could take full advantage of the Lancia's powerful engine. The trip home was much quicker. Before we pulled into town, Carla asked me what I intended to do.

I felt nauseated, bitter, and indignant. My father couldn't possibly have imagined that the Eco T.D.W. was dealing in toxic waste with the Camorra. This was no longer a simple case of small-town fraud. This was "ecomafia." And it was no longer possible to negotiate with those people, it wasn't possible to try to broker a solution to the matter; we had to involve the law.

"We'll go see Mele, and we'll give him the film."

"What about your father?"

I shrugged resignedly. "I'll tell him afterwards."

Mele slammed his hand down hard on the desk. "So you decided to become junior detectives."

"We just wanted to be sure, before we—" I took a stab at self-justification.

"Not a word from you—you're a lawyer, and there are certain things you ought to know already," he scolded. "You've undermined the investigation. They've already cleaned house at the local health board and on Zuglio's land. We won't find any usable evidence to take them to court."

"There are the photographs; there's our own eyewitness testimony," Carla broke in.

"It's not much, barely enough to justify starting an investigation. If the two of you had only been a little smarter, we could have caught them all with their hands in the cookie jar."

"What are you going to do now?"

"I'll make a report to Zan with your statements and the photographs of these gentlemen," he replied. "The first thing we need to figure out is whether this toxic waste operation has anything to do with Giovanna's murder."

"Do you really have to hand over the evidence to Zan?" I asked, though I already knew the answer.

He spread his arms in resignation. "It's his investigation."

Carla and I signed our statement and got up to go.

"Have you told me the whole truth, or should I expect some other surprise later on?" the inspector asked.

Neither of us answered. With a gesture of one hand, the inspector ushered us out of his office.

The secretary informed me that Papa was at the Foundation for a meeting. The Torrefranchi Group was headquartered in a large villa by the river. In the old days, the notables who traveled from the city preferred a boat to the jarring discomfort of a horse-drawn coach. The villa had been built at the orders of a descendant of a Venetian doge at the end of the seventeenth century. Two centuries later, the property had fallen into the hands of a wealthy Jewish family from Trieste. During the Second World War, the villa had been requisitioned by the local German headquarters, and the legitimate owners never returned from Dachau. I had been there on only two occasions with Papa, once for a literary awards ceremony, and once for a charity banquet to raise money to finance the pediatric ward of the new hospital.

At the front gate, I was ordered to halt by two security guards. Muscular physiques wrapped in charcoal-grey tailored suits, with crew cuts and sunglasses. My surname wasn't enough to get me inside. They told me to wait while they requested authorization. After a couple of minutes, they waved me in. At the door, I was welcomed by a courteous secretary in a navy blue suit with a gold-plated name tag on her lapel that identified her as Mariangela. She accompanied me into a comfortable little lounge where she pointed me to a table covered with carafes, coffee pots, and trays of finger pastries. "The meeting is almost over," she told me. "I've already told your father you're here."

About ten minutes passed and a small crowd poured into the lounge. They were too busy talking animatedly and pouring cups of coffee and serving themselves pastries to notice me. Then the Contessa swept in with Davide Trevisan at her heels. Selvaggia kissed me absent-mindedly first on one cheek, then the other. "Your father is still tied up," she warned me in a low voice. Then he headed over to a group of men smoking in a corner.

Trevisan poured himself a glass of fruit juice. "The Contessa has forbidden alcohol," he confided in a whisper.

I was astonished to see him at the Foundation, treated like any of the numerous partners. After his meeting with Papa, I expected to see him kicked out on his ass. But here he sat, safe and happy. He came to sit down in the office chair beside me.

"I have to thank you for your discretion in this matter of the toxic waste," he said in a low voice. "As I explained to your father, I was deceived by several employees who kept the truth from me."

I nodded, doing my best to stay calm. I wanted to tell him that I had photographs of him standing on Zuglio's land as the excavator unearthed the drums, but the Carabinieri would be talking to him about it later.

"We're packing our bags," he added, after biting into a pastry. "We're all heading for Romania. Fuck the Chinese, and fuck the tax collectors."

"Will you still be dealing in waste?"

He smiled with satisfaction. "No. I bought machinery from a bankrupt shoe factory for a song, and I shipped it to Timisoara. Next week, I'm going down to hire the workers." He laid one hand on my arm in a conspiratorial manner. "Twenty female factory workers, all attractive and all available, obviously. In Romania, the real problem is keeping your dick in your pants."

I wondered to myself how I'd ever managed to hang out with such a squalid creature and consider him a friend. I had even thought of asking him to be my best man. Giovanna wouldn't let me. She had always dismissed Davide as a false and conceited fool. So I asked my father to be my best man.

I realized that Trevisan had launched into a description of the joys of Romanian sex, and I decided to put a stop to it by changing the subject. "Of course, there'll be a lot of layoffs here after you leave."

"We'll take the best ones with us," he explained. "We need specialized workers who can teach the others how to do their job. The Romanians don't know how to do a thing."

"What about the others?"

He shrugged. "A lot of them are third-world immigrants, and they can just go back home, because we're sick and tired of blacks and Moroccans." Then he lowered his voice. "And the locals will have to take care of themselves. They'll think of something. Our people have always rolled up their sleeves when times are tough."

Just then, I saw my father walk into the lounge. He came toward me with a smile on his face. "You forgot to shave this morning," he scolded me good-naturedly. "What are you doing here? Did you have something urgent to tell me?"

I smiled in a reassuring manner. "No, Papa. I just wanted to say hello and ask if you'd like to have lunch with me."

"I'm sorry, I already have plans."

"No problem. We'll do it another time."

I drove aimlessly around the countryside for a couple of hours. I couldn't seem to make sense of what had happened. Papa must have had good reasons for what he had done, but I couldn't manage to make sense of his behavior. I couldn't imagine that he had fallen for Trevisan's pathetic lie about being deceived by his employees. Perhaps he had chosen to pretend to believe him, figuring that, in any case, once the Torrefranchi Group had moved to Romania, the problem of the Eco T.D.W. would be unimportant. The real reason I hadn't spoken to him before going to Mele was that, in the end, I knew he'd dissuade me from telling the police anything. But Papa certainly couldn't understand how serious that traffic in toxic waste really was. He hadn't seen the Land of Fires, the plumes of colored smoke befouling the air. People were getting sick and dying because some northeastern manufacturer wanted to save a little money on waste management. My father was probably willing to ignore all that in order to achieve his dream of the Foundation. But I wasn't. Considering the way matters stood, I could be certain of only one thing. I would never work for the Foundation nor would I ever set foot in my father's law offices. Once the Carabinieri's investigation became public, everyone associated with the Torrefranchi Foundation would treat me like a leper. And my father would never forgive me for betraying him. My short professional life in town would be over. After my visit to the Foundation, though, I wasn't so sure that I minded.

Nothing happened for a couple of days. Then one morning Carla came to see me and thrust a sheet of paper into my face. "Read that," she snarled furiously.

I glanced quickly at the first few lines. "You've been fired," I stammered in surprise.

"For entering the laboratory after working hours and for using the equipment for my own personal ends," she recited from memory. "And how do you think they knew about that?"

"From my father," I answered promptly. I looked at her unhappily. "I told him because I wanted to convince him that the pollution caused by the secret waste dump was really serious. Forgive me."

Carla heaved a sigh as she flopped down into a chair. "Oh, they would have gotten rid of me anyway. Ferrari is a powerful man in the world of public health, and if I had reported him he had plenty of strings he could pull."

"If it's any consolation, I'm not in much better shape myself. I'm going to have problems finding clients from now on."

We sat in silence, seated face to face.

"There's something I never told you," she murmured in embarrassment. She stopped, unable to go on. I took one of her hands in both of mine. Carla's hand returned the pressure and she continued with her story. "When I was working in Caserta, they forced me to alter some test results. This helped out a waste management company that was in cahoots with the Camorra. I could say that I was forced to do it, that if I had refused to do it someone else would have done it, for money. But the fact is that I did it. Altering those test results meant that thousands and thousands of acres of pastureland were polluted with toxic substances. It means that I allowed children to drink milk poisoned with dioxin. Children that might very well contract leukemia inside of a year."

I let go of her hand. "That's why Giovanna arranged to bring you up here. And now I understand why you knew so much about the Land of Fires. Why didn't you tell me about at the beginning?"

"I had no obligation to tell you anything."

"Is there anything else I should know?"

Carla didn't answer. She took a new pack of cigarettes out of her purse and opened it with nervous gestures. "Don't take that tone with me," she said, as she brought the flame of her lighter up to the tip of the cigarette. "I'm not Giovanna, get that into your head. I didn't betray you, I never lied to you."

Her words felt to me like a hard punch in the face. I was taking it out on the only person who had had the courage to tell the truth.

"I imagine it wasn't easy to work with those people," I said in an understanding tone.

"I'll say," she responded harshly. "I was twenty-eight years old and I had come down there from the deep north. It didn't take them long to put me in a state of terror. A casual phrase here, a veiled allusion there. That's how they do it. I felt so dirty, so soiled, that I decided that I'd never knuckle under again in my life."

We sat smoking in silence. Then she got up and left without another word. I almost didn't notice that she'd left. I was too busy looking deep inside myself.

* * *

Giacomo Zuglio was brooding as he sat slumped in his easy chair in his living room at home. For a moment, he allowed himself to be distracted by the pathetic spectacle of his sad-sack wife sitting at the dining room table, smoking one cigarette after another, staring into the middle distance. Lucio's arrest, the ensuing loss of reputation in town, and the discovery of the secret toxic dump had wiped away for the moment any dreams he might have had of being admitted into the Foundation. Trevisan hadn't minced words. "I couldn't dream of nominating you right now," Trevisan had told him. Then he'd added that Zuglio would only have to bide his time for a while, let things quiet down. He'd just have to be patient and wait. He hadn't done anything but be patient and wait for the past several years, and he was sick of dealing with messengers and henchmen like Constantin Deaconescu. He wanted a place at the table with the Contessa. The Romanian had warned him that the next day the Carabinieri would conduct a raid on his land and on the headquarters of the Eco T.D.W. and that they would both officially become suspects of conspiracy to traffic in toxic wastes. Nothing to worry about, the Romanian had reassured him. They wouldn't find any significant grounds for indictment, they'd never wind up in court. The trucks and the drivers had already gone back to Romania. He could rely on Constantin. He was a real hardass, and back in Romania, when the Communists had been in charge of things, he had worn the uniform of a captain in the intelligence agency. Zuglio was certain that now he was the right-hand man of the Romanian Mafia in the Northeast, but he had avoided asking any indiscreet questions. Every so often, Constantin had asked him to "invest" certain sums in dollars and marks. Old banknotes stuffed in plastic shopping bags or in black trash bags. That morning Constantin had arranged to meet on a dirt road outside of town.

"You need to get in touch with Barovier and convince him to meet you," he had said.

Zuglio made a face. He had no desire to see Alvise, and he didn't see any reason to do so.

The Romanian had explained the matter to him briefly, and

Zuglio had been frankly impressed with the fiendish brilliance of the plan. Fate was about to play the same trick on Alvise Barovier a second time.

He had extracted his cell phone from the pocket of the heavy jacket and called the motel.

"It's Giacomo Zuglio."

"What do you want?" Barovier had asked, suspiciously.

"I have something to tell you about the old days."

"I'm listening."

"Well, you never learn, do you? These aren't things you talk about on the phone."

Alvise said nothing.

"Well?" he insisted.

"Where and when?"

"This evening at nine, at the trout farm. You remember where it is?"

Zuglio snapped his phone shut with a satisfied smile. It had been easy. Alvise Barovier was an idiot. He always had been.

Zuglio stretched in an easy yawn and looked at his watch. It wasn't long till the meeting. He walked downstairs to the cellar and took a can of wall paint from a shelf. He pried it open with a screwdriver. He pulled a plastic bag out of the paint and rinsed the paint off it in a sink. He ripped open the layers of plastic and checked to make sure that the pistol was loaded. Alvise had a nasty personality. And he was taller and bigger than Zuglio. Better take precautions, like Constantin had warned him. He didn't want to return home that night with a black eye.

* * *

Alvise handed the key in at the reception desk. He climbed onto the stolen bicycle and pedaled off into the night. After a few hundred yards he was already panting. He filled his lungs with cold air to find the strength to keep up his speed. Anxiety had begun to devour him immediately after he hung up. And it kept him from thinking clearly. He couldn't see the absurdity of his thoughts, which were only wish-fulfillments of the yearnings for justice, redemption, and revenge that had tormented him for all these years.

He had spent the last hour walking back and forth across the room. Three steps from the bed to the door, three-and-a-half from the door to the bathroom. He was convinced that Zuglio had finally decided to tell the truth. Or at least that part of the truth that did not involve him personally. After the discovery of the secret toxic waste dump, he must have understood that the only way to stay out of prison was to negotiate on one or several fronts. And now Alvise couldn't wait to meet him face to face. Zuglio would finally clear him of the crime and he would be able to stay here in town to look after Paola and Lucio.

Alvise had never been so confused, weak, and defenseless, but when he looked in the bathroom mirror before leaving the house, he thought he was staring at the face of a winner. Ten minutes later, he reached the trout farm. He leaned the bicycle against the side of Zuglio's Ferrari without a thought for the scratches he'd leave on the bodywork. He pushed the gate open and walked in. The place was empty and silent. Zuglio was waiting for him, leaning against the pole of one of the floodlights that illuminated the walkways between the trout tanks.

"Okay, talk," Alvise snapped.

"What's the hurry?" Zuglio replied sarcastically. "Let me take a good look at you. My goodness, you're in bad shape. Nobody would think that you used to move in high society."

Barovier lost control and grabbed him by the lapels. "You're the reason all this happened to me," he shouted.

Zuglio pulled out his pistol and leveled it at his chest. "Calm down, and get away from me."

Alvise, frightened, took a step back. A cruel smile formed on Zuglio's lips. "You're right. I'm the one who ruined you. But it wasn't my idea."

"Then whose was it?"

"Let's just say people from your social class. They had plans, and you and Conte Giannino didn't fit in with those plans," he answered in amusement. "They weren't interested in your furniture factory, they just wanted to get you out of the way, they wanted a clear playing field. Then they took the whole town for themselves."

In Alvise's befuddled mind there was suddenly a shaft of light, a moment's clarity. He felt like shouting: "Now I understand! Now I've figured it out!" like the town fool. He just had one more question for Zuglio.

"Who killed Giovanna? Was it you?"

Zuglio didn't answer. He just snickered and shook his head. Alvise clenched both fists and took a step forward. The other man aimed the pistol right at his heart. A shot echoed through the silent countryside. The pistol dropped from Zuglio's hand; Zuglio clutched at his chest. He tried to remain standing, but managed only to stumble two steps backward and then toppled into the ice-cold water of a trout tank. Alvise turned suddenly. He saw a man emerge from the darkness.

"I know you," he whispered. "You're the Romanian."

Constantin said nothing. He stepped past him, picked Zuglio's pistol up from the ground, and fired a shot into Alvise's heart. Alvise dropped like a brick. Then the Romanian tossed Zuglio's pistol into the tank, and carefully placed his own pistol into Alvise's dead hand. He wedged his victim's finger into the trigger guard and used it to fire a shot into the air. Then he stood up and looked around with satisfaction. He had always been particularly good at manipulating crime scenes. He walked off thinking to himself that there was nothing left to fear. Zuglio had always been the weak link in the chain. If he had talked, he would have allowed the Carabinieri to reconstruct the hierarchy of the organization that ran the traffic in toxic waste. The only thing that bothered him was that he didn't understand why they had told him to eliminate Alvise Barovier as well.

* * *

At six in the morning the Carabinieri began their sweep. Police seals were placed on the gate outside the toxic waste dump and searches were conducted in the offices of the Eco T.D.W., the financial holding company owned by Zuglio, the Diana nightclub, and the homes of Davide Trevisan, Giacomo Zuglio, and Constantin Deaconescu. None of them was at home. Nor was any compromising evidence found. At 8:20 that morning, Inspector Mele was informed that two corpses had been found at the trout farm. At a little past ten, he called me. "Alvise Barovier is dead," he announced in a formal voice. "He and Zuglio got into a duel and killed one another."

I immediately went to see Carla. I didn't want her to hear about it from the news report on Antenna N/E. She burst into tears and took refuge in my arms. When I got home, I received a phone call from my father.

"I told you he was a killer," he said without preamble. "I don't know how you could have believed him. And I don't know how you could have betrayed my trust."

"I acted according to my conscience, and in the full respect of the law," I shot back. "It's what you taught me to do, Papa."

He ignored my words. "You've shown that you lack the maturity to take on significant professional responsibilities."

"Are you kicking me out of the law firm even before I set foot in it?" I asked, speaking loudly and angrily.

"No, that's hardly called for. I'm just saying that we'll need to reexamine your role. I'm sorry but, at least for moment, you're in no condition to take charge of the law firm."

"At this point, I'm happy to turn down the offer."

"You're going to have to work with me if you hope to get any clients."

"Then I'll just have to do without clients."

"You're behaving like a child," he huffed in annoyance. "I'm trying to be indulgent with you. I know it's only because you're upset about Giovanna's death."

"I don't need your understanding, Papa."

"Try to think clearly, Francesco. And above all, try not to disappoint me."

"Disappoint you? You've disappointed me," I said, snapping the phone shut on him.

On the 1 P.M. news, Beggiolin largely overlooked the significance of the investigation into the toxic waste trafficking. That was not merely because the news was overshadowed by the day's top news item—the deaths of Alvise and Zuglio—but also because cases of fraud of every sort were being discovered on a daily basis by the police. By now, that type of crime was endemic to the Northeast. One need only watch the weekly national broadcast on consumer's rights to see it clearly. Beggiolin read the report with no particular interest or emphasis. He devoted greater attention, on the other hand, to a press release from the Torrefranchi Foundation. The Foundation stated that, while it was completely free of any involvement in the suspected crimes under investigation, it remained willing to clean up the site of the former secret dump, in virtue of its commitment to the environment. Davide Trevisan, through his lawyer, one of my father's assistants, had communicated that he was out of the country on business, and that he would return home as soon as possible to clarify his position.

The special report lasted no longer than two minutes, and the detail that Zuglio had been declared a suspect was overlooked entirely. Then, on the screen, I saw footage of Alvise's corpse prone on the cement. Then I saw Zuglio's body being dragged dripping from the trout tank. The journalist took full advantage of the opportunity to delve into the macabre details, describing how the trout had ravaged the former bank officer's facial features.

Then it was Mele's turn. He refused to make a statement, pointing out that investigations were still underway. Last of all came Zan, who was much more amenable to Beggiolin's questioning. The prosecutor stated that there was no doubt about the reconstruction of what had happened. Barovier and Zuglio had shot one another to death. He was equally confident about the motives. Barovier had nursed a grudge and a deep-seated hatred for Zuglio, since Barovier held Zuglio responsible for his bankruptcy. Probably Barovier had persuaded the former bank officer to meet to thrash out old disagreements, but it had tragically degenerated into a gunfight.

Zan had it all wrong. It wasn't the first time, it wouldn't be the last. Alvise had tried to force destiny to comply with his wishes. He refused to leave town with his tail between his legs, without uncovering the truth that would allow him to begin a new life in town, taking care of Lucio and Paola. He must have obtained a pistol from one of his jailbird friends, and he was convinced that he would be able to force Zuglio to confess. But Zuglio hadn't been born yesterday, and he'd come to the appointment armed as well. I thought that it was better for Alvise that he was dead. If he had won that demented duel, he would have spent the rest of his life in prison after a second, even more humiliating trial. I felt responsible for his death. I had judged him badly, and treated him even worse. I hadn't realized the extent of his desperation.

The phone rang. It was Prunella.

"You see what happens when you try to help Alvise? He's killed again."

"This isn't the time . . ."

"I don't want to have to take care of his funeral. Do you hear me?" she shrieked hysterically.

"According to the law, you're still his wife. And in the eyes of God, as well," I reminded her, with a touch of malice. "Anyway, don't worry about it. I'll take care of everything."

I washed my face. And then I phoned Zan.

"Has Lucio Zuglio been informed of the deaths of his two fathers?"

"I don't think so. I was planning to send Inspector Mele to report the news to him."

"I'd like to do it, if that's possible."

"No problem. Drop by the court building to pick up the authorization for a visit."

In the hospital I showed the paper with the prosecutor's signature to the detention officer outside Lucio's room. Lucio was flat on his back in a special bed designed for trauma victims. He was in bad shape, but the doctors had declared that he was no longer in danger. He looked at me with curiosity.

"I know you," he managed to say. His upper lip had been stitched all the way up to the base of the nose, and he was missing two of his bottom front teeth. "You're Francesco Visentin."

I pulled up a chair and sat by the side of the bed. "I have some bad news for you."

He squinted unhappily. "I know all about it," he said quickly. "The nurses told me."

"I'm sorry you had to find out like that."

"They were happy to give me bad news," he commented. "Here everyone hates me."

He reached out with one hand and took a glass off the night table. He carefully inserted the straw into his mouth. "I don't give a crap about that asshole. My home life was pure hell," he went on. "But I am sort of sorry about Alvise. He was crazy, there's no doubt about that. But he was okay, you know. He'd come to visit me, and talk and talk about taking me back to Argentina with him. Didn't anybody ever tell him how many years I'm going to spend in prison?"

The boy was striking poses. He wanted to seem like a gangster in the movies, but he was pathetic.

"I'd like to take your case, be your defense lawyer."

He looked at me suspiciously. "Why?"

"Alvise asked me to."

He shrugged. "Fine by me. You'd be better than the court-appointed lawyer, that's for sure."

"How did you meet Giovanna?" I asked him suddenly.

He made a grimace that looked vaguely like a smile. "One day she waited outside my school and introduced herself. That's all."

"How did she find out you were brother and sister?"

"Someone told her. But I don't know who."

"How many times did you see her?"

"I don't know, three or four times. We would meet in a restaurant in Treviso."

I stood up and moved the chair back to the wall. "I'll be back to bring you papers to sign, naming me as your defense lawyer."

"I'm worried about my mother," he said. "She's an alcoholic and she needs treatment."

"I'll talk to family services."

"Papa—I mean Zuglio—had a sizable chunk of money set aside. Momma can afford to go to a private clinic."

"I'll see what I can do," I promised.

I stuck my hand out. He gripped it. "I'm sorry about Giovanna," he said softly.

I gave him a quick, formal smile, and I turned to leave.

"I saw her that night," he whispered uncertainly.

I turned on my heel. "The night of the murder?"

He nodded. "I was driving around with the guys and I saw her park her car in the front driveway of a house."

"What time was it?"

"It must have been one."

"You're wrong. At that time of night she was at home, in bed with her lover."

"It was Giovanna. I'm certain of it," he replied firmly. "Then, around four-thirty I came back by and her car was still there."

I shook my head in annoyance. "Don't talk nonsense," I warned him harshly. "Giovanna was already dead by four-o'clock."

Lucio puffed out his cheeks in irritation. "They're wrong about the time. If you don't believe me, ask the Contessa."

"What does Selvaggia have to do with it?"

"I saw her Mercedes drive out of the mansion."

* * *

"Filippo! What are you doing in the dark!" Selvaggia had entered the studio like a gust of wind. She'd turned on the light and strode across the big room, busily opening the shutters covering the three big windows, allowing daylight to flood into the room.

Filippo didn't move from the stool where he sat, staring at his finished sculpture.

"It's done, what do you think of it?" asked Filippo as he sat contemplating the sculpture.

Selvaggia gave the sculpture a quick and distracted glance and said only: "What a waste of time. Like the time you waste trying to drag me into Giovanna's murder."

Filippo smiled. "The great Moroncini truly has an unusual idea of professional confidentiality."

"Careful Filippo, don't push me."

"Or you'll do what?" This was the first time that he'd challenged her so openly.

He wasn't expecting his mother's reaction: she began to chuckle, quietly at first, and then harder and harder, finally in uncontrolled and raucous gales of laughter.

"Oh, you really are an idiot," she said, as she laughed.

Then she left the studio, leaving the door open behind her.

Filippo stood up. He closed the shutters again. He walked over to the main switch and turned off the overhead lights. He clumped back across the room, limping across the space he knew by heart, and sat down on his work stool, in front of the sculpture. Running his fingers along the wire, he found the push-switch that controlled the spotlight focused on the sculpture. With a constant, obsessive rhythm, he began turning it on and off, on and off.

CLICK. CLACK. Dark. Light.

The sculpture was finished. And she hadn't even looked at it. Dark. Light.

There the sculpture sat, before him. A smooth, white, waxen mother.

He need only push his thumb on the switch and his mother disappeared. Another click and that chilly, funereal image returned to weigh him down.

The darkness was comforting. The light was distressing.

The work of the past year was finished, and there was nothing left to be done, no way to improve on it.

"A waste of time," she'd called it.

There was nothing left to do but destroy it. Or transform it. Create a new sculpture. A rebirth from his mother's dead body. From a portrait of his mother to a self-portrait.

Light. He needed to bring light. Enough with running away. Enough with chasing the one who had always escaped him.

He needed to use the red-hot iron to carve deep within himself. Without subterfuges. Without extenuating circumstances.

He'd start from the external wounds, and then he'd dig down to remove the internal ones.

Reshape himself, without fear. Out of the darkness.

He'd start from the bottom, from his fractured femur. Then, as soon as he felt ready, he would carve into the right cheek. Then he'd venture into the slight deviation of the nasal septum. He'd shrink the eyes and reshape the hair. He'd eliminate the breasts and round out the biceps. Wrists and ankles could remain as they were, slender and elegant.

A metamorphosis. A passage from death to life.

Dark. Light. Her. Him. With iron and with fire.

Not a son anymore.

To work.

Light. And then? Dark.

* * *

The house described by Lucio was a small but elegant one-story building, set at the center of a broad lawn and surrounded by a towering and impenetrable boxwood hedge. You couldn't see anything from the street, and it had taken a considerable effort just to find the driveway. I stepped out of my car and walked over to the front door. I rang the bell, even though I was certain there was no one inside. I walked around the house, trying to peep in through the wooden shutters, but they were shut tight. Lucio's story made no sense. He couldn't possibly have seen Giovanna the night of the murder; it must have been the night before, or a few nights before. And what would she be doing there with the Contessa? They couldn't stand the sight of one another, and they certainly had no reason to be socializing at night. But, if the boy was telling the truth, I might finally be looking at the house in the video. That was why I did not hesitate to slip a heavy-duty screwdriver between the two panels of one of the shutters. The wood strained and then cracked open with a sharp sound. Behind it was a window covered by filmy curtains that blocked my view. I had no choice but to force it open in turn. The sound of an alarm siren split the air. After an initial moment of panic, I recovered my nerves and pushed the window open. I immediately recognized the cupboard, the kitchen table, and the chairs. And the door that Giovanna had shut in the camera's face. I heard her voice repeating: "Come on, cut it out."

"I found you, you bastard," I shouted, louder than the wailing alarm.

The officer on desk duty informed me that this was the inspector's day off. I told him that I urgently needed to speak with him, but it was only after insisting at length, and only with great reluctance, that he told me that I could find him at the bocce lanes at a certain tavern down by the river.

Mele was playing a team bocce match. He was on the same team as the town barber. His adversaries were ahead, with two bocce balls practically glued to the little boccino ball. After talking it over with his teammate, he took a short run-up to the line and then hurled the bocce ball in a low flat arc that sent the boccino whizzing against the far wall.

I called his name. He came over, cleaning his hands on his handkerchief. "Every so often I come here to teach the Venetians how to play," he joked. Then he noticed how tense I was. "What's up?"

I pulled Giovanna's digital camera out of my pocket. "I have something to show you."

Mele said goodbye to his friends, to a chorus of objections at the interruption to the match. We climbed into his car. I showed him the video and told him about Lucio and the house in the suburbs.

"You say you set off the alarm?"

"Yes."

"Then someone must have broken in, I take it?"

"Certainly, it was me."

He grabbed me by the arm. "We have no idea who broke in," he corrected me. "All we know is that a crime may have been committed. For all we know, the burglars are still inside the house."

"Inspector, I don't understand," I blurted out impatiently.

He smiled. "If we think of it that way, then there's no need to ask the prosecutor for a search warrant."

"Are you saying you don't trust Zan?"

Mele didn't answer. "Go to the house and wait for me there. I'm going to run by the barracks and get an agent from the forensic office."

"But why? All we need to do is find out who owns the house and we'll know the murderer's name."

"No, that's not enough. Now we're going to do things my way."

The alarm had stopped wailing. The sergeant from the forensic office slipped on a pair of latex gloves, stepped in through the window that I had forced open, and unlocked the front door for the two of us.

"I disconnected the alarm," he announced.

"Don't touch anything, Francesco," the inspector warned me.

The house was completely empty, except for the furniture. The expert from the forensic office only managed to find a few blurry fingerprints. "Inspector, this place has been cleaned professionally."

"Let's take a look at the bathroom," said Mele.

The sergeant pulled out a long narrow pair of steel tweezers and began reaching down into the bathtub drain. He managed to extract a few long blonde hairs and placed them carefully into a clear plastic bag.

"Do you think that's Giovanna's hair?" I asked.

He nodded confidently. "I think she was killed here."

"Here? But her body was found in the bathtub in her house."

"But there were no fingerprints other than yours, Giovanna's, and the cleaning woman's. In order to erase his own fingerprints, the killer would have had to erase yours as well. That was the first piece of evidence that aroused my suspicions," he explained. "And then there was another detail. The bathwater found in her lungs contained bath salts that didn't match the ones found at her house. And there were minor abrasions on her heels, as if the body had been dragged for several yards."

"I don't understand why the killer would have run such risks to take Giovanna's body back to her house."

"We're dealing with a smart but careless murderer," he said. "He tried to convince us that Giovanna was the victim of a mishap, but he committed a series of errors."

Then I suddenly remembered an important detail. "If Giovanna was killed here, then it means that Lucio told the truth about the Contessa, too."

"We'll see about that," he grunted. "Though it strikes me as unlikely. What was she doing here with Giovanna and her lover? Having an orgy?"

I had another theory, but this wasn't the time to talk about it. "Are you going to tell Zan about this?" I asked.

"I don't think so," he replied. "First I want to find out the results of the tests on the hair samples. In the meanwhile, I'm going to find out who owns this house and do some discreet investigating. I want to present an airtight report."

"Discreet investigations are also slow investigations," I commented.

"It's been more than a month and a half since the murder. Another day or two won't change a thing," he replied. "The important thing is to catch the killer."

The sergeant did his best to repair the shutter that I had forced open, and we left the house.

"I don't need to tell you not to speak to anyone about all this. I'll get in touch with you as soon as I find out something," said Mele. Then he pulled the digital camera out of his jacket pocket and extended it to me. "We don't need to include this in the official evidence. At least for the moment."

I smiled in gratitude and got into my car.

* * *

Antonio Visentin wasn't very happy with Selvaggia's latest maneuver. They weren't handling their children right at all. Professor Moroncini's report laid out a clinical picture that made Filippo out to be little more than an idiot with no independent judgment, a danger to himself and therefore to society at large.

The appointment with the local magistrate who would order the interdiction if he found just cause was set for the following morning, and Visentin had decided to make a last attempt with Filippo, even though he knew it would spur Selvaggia's wrath. But in Visentin's eyes, their children offered the sole possibility of living on after one's own death, and continuing through them into the future. To have Filippo interdicted would mean chopping off the deepest roots, breaking off the continuity through family inheritance that had allowed their families to rule and flourish through all the twists and turns of history, through all the political regimes. Every political and social transformation in the history of the Northeast had been guided and controlled by their families. And Selvaggia could not fully understand this. For the first time, he had sensed the depth of the difference between them. An ocean as vast as the dozens of generations that had resulted in Antonio Visentin. Selvaggia was violating the only true taboo: the hereditary taboo. And Visentin felt obliged to prevent her from breaking it. For all the transformations sweeping the Northeast, the power of the families must remain intact. Otherwise, it would be the beginning of the end for all of them.

When he saw him come into his studio, Filippo hastily threw a white sheet over the sculpture he was working on. Visentin discussed the topic tactfully, explaining the legal and psychological consequences of interdiction, the mark of shame that this legal act would stamp on the name of the Calchi Renier family. They were the same arguments that he had attempted to use on Selvaggia, but to no effect. He was surprised and disappointed to see Filippo's obedient, even passive attitude.

"I've always done what my mother told me to do," he had answered. "If this is what my mother wants, so be it. All things considered, I don't really care either way."

The venerable old lawyer had insisted, he'd spoken to him like a father, but Filippo had closed down, shutting himself up in a mute obstinacy that had persuaded the lawyer that Selvaggia might well be right. With Filippo, sole heir to the Calchi Renier fortune, the dynasty was on the verge of extinction. Selvaggia had told him about Filippo's latest act of folly. The Contessa had arranged for a date between her son and Isabella Beghin, a girl of unusual beauty and a tractable personality, the daughter of the Beghin family that owned the tanneries. You might say that Selvaggia had selected her genetically. But during their first date, Filippo had convinced her that he had barely a year left to live. The girl had fled without a backward glance, after earnestly advising Filippo to seek medical help overseas. By now, Filippo lived in an isolation that bordered on the autistic. How could she entrust her son with business responsibilities if he accused his mother of being an accomplice to murder? And, in the end, Visentin had left that gloomy studio persuaded that, after all, interdiction was the only reasonable solution.

Visentin was growing confused about everything, about what was right and what was wrong. Maybe Selvaggia had been right when, during their last argument about Filippo, she had called him the biggest hypocrite in the land of the hypocrites, and had then added: "You and I are a perfect pair of carnivores: a lioness and a jackal, and what he have in common is our love for gazelles."

The only difference between them was that Selvaggia had no hesitation in saying it, while it frightened him even to think it.

* * *

Inspector Mele had nothing to report for three long days. Three days of intolerable anxiety. Then he showed up late on the third night. It had been snowing for a few hours. Fresh wet snow that didn't stick to the ground. When I was a little boy, the snow lasted for a whole week.

"That hair came from Giovanna's head and body," he announced, removing his wet heavy jacket. "And we found traces of the same bath salts that were found in her lungs. There's no doubt about it: she was killed in that house."

"Any information about who owns it?"

"A company headquartered in the Principality of Monaco," he replied disappointedly.

"And what would a company in Monaco want with a house here in town?"

"The company is nothing more than a front for tax evasion and moving money around without interference. The right question to ask is who, here in town, can make use of such a complex network of shell companies?"

"The Torrefranchi Foundation," I whispered.

"The house belongs to the Foundation, Francesco. And that points back to the Contessa, once again. I went back to question Lucio again, and I'm convinced that, if nothing else, he really did see her car that night."

"Do you think she's involved in the murder?"

"I couldn't say. But I did wonder how Giovanna's dead body was moved from the little suburban villa to her house. At first, I assumed that the murderer must have used Giovanna's Mazda, but the forensic examinations rule that out."

"He must have used his own car. Or else the Contessa's Mercedes," I responded.

"The Contessa's car was one of the hypotheses, based on Lucio's testimony. I decided to check it out, and I discovered that after the murder she got a new car. And a new chauffeur." The inspector stood up, walked over to the liquor tray, and poured himself a shot of vintage marsala. "At that point, I got curious, and I found out that the chauffeur was a Romanian, a certain Toader Tomusa who had been in an Italian prison. The day after he was released from prison, he was hired by the Contessa."

"Everyone knows that Selvaggia has been underwriting a project to reintegrate ex-convicts into civilian society."

"What a philanthropist she is," he commented sarcastically. "And don't you find it odd that, at every turn in this case, a Romanian pops up? Constantin Deaconescu, his employees at the Club Diana, and the employees of the Eco T.D.W. were all Romanians."

"Mafia?" I guessed.

He nodded. "Like all the other organizations, it has operations here in the Northeast. This is the perfect place to launder money, by investing in legal activities. Go into any bar and you'll find plenty of entrepreneurs ready to do a little business, without worrying about their partners' criminal records."

I nodded back. Things were becoming very clear. "The Torrefranchi Group is about to move its operations to Romania,"

I confided. "They've built a new industrial site on the outskirts of Timisoara."

From the surprised expression on his face, I understood that the inspector knew nothing about the Foundation's plans. He gulped down his marsala and pulled on his heavy jacket.

"What do you plan to do now?"

"Without some new piece of evidence, my investigation ends here."

"Are you joking? If you don't trust Zan, go to the chief prosecutor: he'll listen to you."

"It would mean flushing what little we've uncovered down the toilet," he answered brusquely. "Zan and the district attorney are both respectable people, it's just that . . ." He broke and tried to find the right words. "They both have a natural inclination to be both benevolent and secretive when it comes to the Foundation. I can't go to them and say that I suspect the Contessa of being an accomplice to murder. They'd take me for a madman and she'd know all about it two minutes later."

"Then let's unleash a scandal. We'll contact the national press."

"The Foundation is the most important industrial group in the area. The various member companies spend a fortune on newspaper advertising. I'm afraid the business considerations involved will outweigh Giovanna's death."

"I'm not going to just stand by and watch," I announced in a bellicose tone of voice.

"I couldn't agree with you more. But you have more of a chance of finding the truth than I do."

"But how?"

"Your father. I have no doubt that he is deeply involved in Foundation business, but I remember him coming into Giovanna's house after her body was found. He was overwhelmed with grief; I can't believe he's willing to look the other way."

Mele slipped out the door soundlessly. He had a point. Papa would never allow Giovanna's murderer to go unpunished, but at the same time he would never willingly lift a finger against his own class. We had to put his back to the wall so that he'd be forced to act. There could be only one explanation for the presence of the Contessa at the little house: the killer was Filippo. I had never mentioned it to the inspector because of the reciprocal alibi that Filippo and I had provided for one another. That was a mistake, and I would have to rectify it at my earliest opportunity. I had eliminated Filippo from the list of suspects because I didn't want to believe that Giovanna had resumed making love with him. But now that I thought about it, the phrase "I became the slut of the man who ruined my life" could still make sense with reference to Filippo. He had nearly killed himself after she left him to be with me. Giovanna had been wracked by guilt over the car crash, and he had never tired of tormenting her and fanning the flames of that guilt. When he came to the Club Diana to talk to me, he must already have murdered her. He had made sure people saw him so that he could construct an alibi while his mother and the chauffeur moved the body and set up the false murder scene.

The next morning I couldn't shave. My hands were shaking too badly. I had spent the night trying to figure out the best way to approach my father about this, but I had only been able to string together an endless series of tangled ideas. For my entire life, I had considered Papa to be the finest man alive. I had always considered myself lucky to have him as a mentor, in life and in my profession. After Giovanna's death, day by day, that image had been shattered into smithereens. Once justice had been served and Filippo and Selvaggia were indicted for Giovanna's murder, I would make a clean and lasting break from him and from his corrupt world. The thing that made me especially sad was my awareness that it would be a relief for him as well. I wasn't the son he wanted. He wanted a son who was willing to sacrifice himself and his ideals on the altar of success and business interests without turning a hair. I was all too familiar with Papa's moral justifications. Antonio Visentin, the great lawyer, the finest of them all, only advised his clients in their own best interests. If, after that, his clients chose to break the law, it was none of his concern. His objective was only to safeguard the interests of his client. But a client like the Foundation had ties to the Romanian Mafia, was polluting the environment, and had committed who could say how many other crimes—and he couldn't ignore that. That was why I was breaking off my relationship with Papa. He had always shown me the clean and rigorous aspect of the profession; he must have assumed that, with the passage of time and the disenchantment that comes with experience, I would accept the dirty side of the law as well. But that's not what happened. We had disappointed one another, we had judged one another badly. I left my house determined to outdo the great lawyer, to outsmart him and force him to the bargaining table. Words like "father" and "son" no longer had any meaning.

For the first time, when I walked into the law office, I felt like a stranger, despite the fondness and sympathy of the secretaries. My father gave me a chilly greeting. I was grateful to him for that. An affectionate gesture would have undermined my determination.

I was brief and to the point. I told him about the suburban house, the evidence, Filippo, and the Contessa, and I waited for him to react. At first, he turned ashen, but then he recovered, and at the end he sneered, a hostile lawyer ready to demolish a witness.

"So you're suggesting that Filippo is the murderer, and Selvaggia is actually his accomplice," he began, sarcastically. "I never realized you had such a lively imagination and such a faulty memory. Allow me to remind you that Filippo is your alibi . . ."

The time had come to administer the fatal blow. "There is an eyewitness who saw the Contessa's Mercedes leave the little suburban house at four-thirty in the morning." Of course, I neglected to tell him that the eyewitness was Lucio, or he'd have simply enjoyed a hearty laugh at my expense and then asked me to leave his office.

He was speechless. Only for an instant, the time it took to turn the news over in his mind. "And all this witness saw was Selvaggia's car?" he asked in an icy voice.

"That's right."

"Has he already made a statement?"

"Not yet. First I wanted to come to terms with you."

"What do you want?"

"Filippo's confession."

He ran a hand over his face and then stared me right in the eye, thinking. "As we speak, Filippo is in court," he said after a while, in a neutral tone of voice. "He is being interviewed by the magistrate, who is deliberating whether or not to accept Selvaggia's request to have him declared incompetent. There is no doubt that the request will be accepted."

"Well, well, what a remarkable coincidence," I interrupted.

He ignored my words. "Even if he really is guilty, which I do not believe, you need to keep in mind that, once he has been declared incompetent, Filippo will never be sent to prison. It will be a walk in the park to have him declared temporarily insane at the time of the commission of the murder."

"I know that very well. And I am not interested in having an unfortunate lunatic sent to prison. I just want justice."

"That would mean dragging Selvaggia into criminal court as well."

"Along with her former chauffeur," I added. "As accomplices to murder."

He bared his teeth in a grimace. "Even as inexperienced and naïve a lawyer as you would manage to win an acquittal," he shot back, with an edge. "You would have to give up your alibi, and testimony provided nearly two months after the fact is certainly questionable. And that's not counting the fact that you would have to find some way of proving that Giovanna's corpse was inside the Mercedes. Do you think that you could find a prosecutor willing to base an indictment on such a flimsy accusation?"

"Filippo killed her," I snarled. "Do you want him to get away with it?"

"No. The problem is that, no matter what, Selvaggia cannot be dragged into this."

"What would you suggest?"

"If he's guilty, and I repeat, that remains to be seen, we will have him committed to a clinic where he will remain as long as it takes for him to be cured, no longer capable of harming others or himself."

I stood up. "I'm disgusted," I said flatly. "All you care about is making sure that Selvaggia is safe."

"I want to make sure that a respectable individual is not publicly defamed."

I refrained from commenting on his positive characterization of Selvaggia. I was too demoralized. My father had knocked me down, and I lacked the strength to get back on my feet. Everything he had said was true. Once again, I had misjudged the evidence in my possession. He had offered me the possibility of an out-of-court settlement between families, but I still preferred the kind of justice you get from a court. I didn't waste my breath telling him so. He would just have laughed in my face.

I took refuge at Carla's house, and told her everything that had happened. She lit a cigarette and went to the window to smoke, with her back to me.

"Have you looked at the newspaper?" she asked after a while.

"No. I was thinking about other things."

She picked up the day's paper from the table and handed it to me. "Threat to the Generational Change of the Guard in Local Corporate Leadership," was the headline at the top of page one of the business section. Industrial and trade associations in the Northeast were all expressing their concern at the inability of the scions of the leading families to take over the companies their fathers had founded. A noted psychiatrist had been invited to lecture on the topic. According to the psychiatrist, these young people had grown up certain that they would be successful, and now they were unable to deal with the economic downturn.

"The leading families are in crisis. So?" I asked.

"It's the end of the leading families," Carla specified. "At least here in town. Neither you nor Filippo will be carrying on the family tradition and your parents are leaving for Romania, taking companies and cash with them."

"Maybe that's not such a negative thing," I commented.

"There'll be nothing but rubble and garbage left behind."

I read aloud the last few lines from the interview with the psychiatrist, who announced his optimism—the people of this part of the world were accustomed to rolling up their sleeves and starting over.

"Of course. The legend of the hard-headed, hard-working people of the Northeast," she said sarcastically. "People like your father and the Contessa did what they wanted to do, and no one is going to ask them to pay."

"What do you mean?"

"That you shouldn't be surprised when you find out that Selvaggia isn't going to be indicted. And that justice will never be done for Giovanna's murder. Around here, that's not how things work."

"Should I just give up?"

She shrugged and didn't answer.

While I was on my way home, the Contessa's Mercedes pulled up next to me; she waved to me to stop. I pulled into a store's parking area and got out of my car. Selvaggia only lowered her window.

"Giovanna was nothing but a little whore and she got what she deserved," she hissed in a chilly voice.

"Is that why Filippo killed her?" I asked, doing my best to maintain my calm.

"It wasn't Filippo and I've never set foot in that mansion. That night I was at home."

"I trust you implicitly," I shot back sarcastically.

"Remember that if I go down, you all come with me. Your father first and foremost."

The car window slid silently up and the Mercedes moved away.

I was trembling with fury when I got back in my car. I calmed down in a few minutes and tried to think about what had happened. Selvaggia's furious reaction and her final remark might mean she didn't feel all that safe after all. Perhaps it was worth trying to find evidence to nail her. After all, I had nothing left to lose.

* * *

At the interdiction hearing, Filippo had answered every question, without hesitation. When he was asked how much he thought Villa Selvaggia might be worth, he had confidently replied, "One euro," and so on.

His mother could rightly be proud of him. Perhaps she was celebrating in his psychiatrist's bed.

After leaving the courts building, Filippo went to a hardware store and purchased a length of high-quality rope, the strongest in the store. Then, to make sure he did things right, he went to the only bookshop in town and purchased a handbook on the art of tying knots. And now there he was, sitting in his studio, in the company of his own self-portrait in wax, which seemed to be staring at him indulgently.

While he coiled one end of the rope into an "S," he saw everything, for the first time, in a different light. His mother, the magistrate, and Professor Moroncini all appeared to him as characters in a farce—each of them playing two roles. At the hearing, they had enacted a sort of macabre ballet. They had overwhelmed him with embarrassed wheedling and coaxing, and he had been reminded of that painting by Edvard Munch in which men and women seem to be moving toward the viewer like so many unsuspecting corpses out for a stroll. They were certainly dead, and yet they continued to strive, contrive, and conspire as if the world had just come into existence, as if nothing had existed before them. They were convinced they were unique, indestructible, and immortal. And yet they thought that the crazy one—the one who was incapable of understanding the difference between right and wrong—was him!

"Start with an 'S'-shaped length of rope, leaving plenty of extra length extending off the bottom. Keep wrapping tight coils spiraling up the outside until you're satisfied, then tuck the end of the rope through the top eye," he read from the manual. He followed the directions closely.

Put an end to it. This was the only possible form of liberty.

At first, he had thought of doing it in the bathtub. But that had seemed to be in poor taste, considering how poor Giovanna had died. And then a hanging was more spectacular, it provided a touch of the artistic. And that was why he had been carefully studying the handbook for the past hour. The book was balanced on his music stand.

He enjoyed reading and rereading the straightforward instructions: "This is a very practical, strong, and secure noose, but may become difficult to untie if pulled hard." Excellent. It was as if the anonymous author of the manual was perfectly aware of the macabre use to which his instructions would be put and was trying to remain detached, to keep from feeling any involvement in a murder or a suicide. Because that was the obvious use of a noose, or a slipknot, or, of course, a hangman's knot.

He would certainly have given anything to see his mother's face when she made the discovery. How would she react to the rebellion of her little puppet? Who would she call? The butler? Visentin? Or would she cut the rope herself? He felt pretty sure that she was capable of doing it. No one was as strong as she was. What about Moroncini? If the professor suddenly found himself without clients, Filippo wouldn't have minded a bit.

He wrapped one more loop to complete the noose. He slid it up and down along the sliding rope. He widened the noose and slipped his head into it. He slid the noose up until he could feel the rope tighten around his neck. He pulled his head out of the noose, checked the length, and pulled on it several times to test its spring. It was a perfect, nine-loop noose. The classical seven loops suggested in the manual struck him as too few. Nine seemed safer somehow. Now he only had to wait for the right day.

Just then, he realized that his cell phone had been ringing for a while. It must be his mother. These days, she was the only who ever called him. When he picked up the phone, he planned to mute it, but he noticed that there was another number on the display. Curious, he pushed the green button to answer.

* * *

After my run-in with Selvaggia, I felt sure if I wanted to get anywhere, I'd have to take advantage of Filippo's psychological instability. Without any specific plan, I picked up my cell phone and searched for his name in the phone book.

He answered after an endless series of rings.

"Your mother is going to have you locked up in a lovely clinic, and you won't get out again until you're old and senile," I said in a burst of words.

"I don't see why she would want to do that," he replied, unperturbed.

"She and my father want to avoid a trial in criminal court, because she would be found guilty as your accomplice."

"What are you talking about?"

"Have you already forgotten you murdered Giovanna?"

Filippo said nothing. I tried to provoke him further by telling him how he had killed Giovanna in the little suburban house and how his mother had gotten rid of the body.

Filippo huffed in annoyance. "You're barking up the wrong tree. My mother had me declared incompetent because I told my analyst she was a murderer," he explained, and then clicked off.

"Filippo said those exact words?" Inspector Mele demanded.

"That's right," I answered.

"That makes no sense," he commented. "And that boy isn't all there, mentally. They had good reason to have him declared incompetent."

"Selvaggia hated Giovanna. Maybe she found out that Filippo was sleeping with her, and she went to the mansion after her son left, and then drowned her, with the help of her chauffeur."

Mele raised his hands in a gesture of surrender. "First you tell me it was Filippo, now it was his mother with her chauffeur," he cried. "The only thing we know for sure is that Giovanna was killed in the mansion and a couple of hours later Lucio saw the Contessa's Mercedes drive out the front gate." The inspector flashed a satisfied smile. "By the way, I found the Mercedes," he announced in a triumphant tone. "The chauffeur had paid a wrecker from Pordenone with a criminal record as long as your arm to demolish it, but instead of crushing the car he kept it. He planned to sell it somewhere outside of the country, but my colleagues found it during a routine check."

"At last, a little luck," I commented.

"And that's not all," he continued, with even greater satisfaction. "I immediately sent the sergeant from the forensic office to do some tests. He found an entire handprint on a metal surface. It was Giovanna's. What probably happened is the arm flopped out of the blanket or tarp the body was wrapped in."

"Then we've got them."

"Let's just say that this is a substantial step forward," he replied cautiously. "Enough to indict the chauffeur but not the Contessa. And the Romanian left town some time ago, we'll never track him down. We have to find a way of linking Selvaggia to the murder."

"How can we do it?"

"The phone records. For her home phone and her cell phone," he answered. "If her son called her for help after murdering Giovanna, we'll find a record of it. It's not conclusive evidence, but together with the testimony on the car, it would be enough to force the prosecutor to name her as a suspect."

"But to obtain the phone records, you'd need the authorization of the court, wouldn't you?" I objected.

"That's certainly true for me. But not for you . . ."

In the middle of the afternoon of the following day I walked into the men's room of a multiplex cinema outside Padua for a meeting with a guy who would hand over the Contessa's phone records. I had no idea who he was. Mele had organized everything. The guy had told me to bring him an envelope with five thousand euros in cash and to forget I had ever seen his face. The signal of recognition was a navy blue scarf hanging out of my overcoat pocket. When I walked in, there were two people washing their hands. A young man and a middle-aged man, about forty, with a buzz cut. I started washing my hands, too. The young man left immediately. The older man dried his hands methodically, waiting for me to do the same. Then he pulled an envelope out of his pocket and extended it. I handed over the cash. He took the time to check the contents of the envelope, and then he left. I walked into a stall, sat down on the toilet, and opened the envelope. It contained two sheets of paper. One was for the phone in Villa Selvaggia, but there were no phone calls between 9 P.M. and 8:30 the following morning. The records for her cell phone on the other hand showed numerous phone calls until 11 P.M. Then there was nothing until 3:26 A.M. When I read the area code I was disappointed at first, because it wasn't the same as Filippo's cell phone. Then I focused on the number and it dawned on me. I knew who had killed Giovanna. I punched in the number. The murderer picked up on the fourth ring.

"It was you," I accused him.

My father said nothing. Then he hung up.

* * *

Selvaggia was having dinner with a Bulgarian businessman. She was about to palm off a collection of old industrial machinery on him. It was all junk, good for scrap and nothing more. In the middle of dinner, Antonio had called to warn her that Francesco had discovered the truth.

How could that have happened? How had he learned the

truth? She had never been confronted with an ineluctable sequence of events before. She had always had the time to calculate, control, and manipulate. For the first time, a hint of panic had begun to surge in her chest. It was a horrible sensation; she would have to make sure it didn't get out of control.

She left the restaurant and ordered her driver to take her home. She barely had time to take off her evening gown, put on something comfortable, empty her office safe of cash and documents, and toss everything into a valise. She raced upstairs. She threw open one door after another, until she arrived in Filippo's bedroom. Her son wasn't there. She looked into the bathroom: empty. "He must be in his studio," she thought with annoyance, and she raced back down the stairs.

The door to the studio was closed. On the door handle hung a sign reading "Do Not Disturb," decorated with a hand-drawn skull, by Filippo of course. Selvaggia angrily threw open the door to the studio and called his name loudly, as if she wanted to scold him for everything that was happening. There was no answer. The room was dark. She flicked on the light switch, took a step forward, and stared in shock. She dropped her purse and clapped her hands over her mouth to suffocate a shriek of horror. In the corner, over the worktable, her son's body was hanging from a noose at the end of a rope dangling from a wooden rafter. He was dressed in his sculptor's smock. His face was shrouded in shadow, and his legs were hidden behind a screen. Filippo. Her legs trembling, Selvaggia found the strength to walk over to the lifeless body, dangling like a sack hauled up off the floor. She edged around the screen and forced herself to look up. What she saw left her breathless: dangling from the rope was not Filippo but a perfect wax likeness of him, the sculpture that depicted him faithfully. The effect was horrifying and mocking, just as its derisive creator had hoped.

Selvaggia gasped in astonishment, and from her open mouth there issued a roar that had something ancestral about it, like the furious impotence of the roar of a wild animal that had been dealt a fatal blow.

* * *

Sitting in his empty train compartment, Filippo had the sensation that Selvaggia's roar had echoed through his ears. Of course, that was impossible, he couldn't even guess what time his mother would return home. Sometimes, though, our imagination can put us in touch with something profoundly real.

For the first time in his life he had done everything with mathematical precision. He had closed the curtains of the studio, positioned the mannequin in just the right shaft of light, made the final minor adjustments to the staging, fastened the placard to the door handle, knowing that only his mother would be arrogant enough to disturb him. Then he stepped out the door, making sure no one noticed his departure, and walked to the train station in forty minutes. The day before, he had gone to the bank and emptied his personal savings account, transferring the other funds to a Swiss bank, the way Counselor Visentin had shown him. The interdiction had not yet taken effect, and they would not be able to move fast enough to block the transfer.

There were still people in the train station, for the most part commuters returning home. His was the only empty compartment. He looked at his watch. Just three minutes to scheduled departure time.

The door of the compartment slid open. Filippo saw a pretty girl step through, with long, smooth, black hair. She was bundled up in a heavy shearling jacket and she was laboriously pushing a huge imitation-Vuitton suitcase.

"Is this seat free?" she asked Filippo without even glancing at him.

Filippo answered lazily, gesturing with one hand at the empty seat across from him.

The girl tried to lift the heavy suitcase up to the luggage rack. After the second effort, she gave up, and hoisted it onto the seat next of her.

"As long as no one else needs the seat," she half-heartedly justified her actions, more to herself than to Filippo.

Filippo merely nodded. He hadn't expected to share his journey with anyone else. And he was embarrassed to display his limp. For no particular reason, he asked: "Where are you headed?"

The girl looked at him for the first time. She didn't seem any more interested in conversations with strangers on a train than he did. Still, she replied, either out of good manners, or because she hoped that Filippo would help her put her suitcase up on the rack: "Anywhere, anywhere that's far from here."

Filippo nodded again, shyly. It was a good answer. The right answer. He wished that "Anywhere" was the name of a place. Anywhere, Elsewhere, Faraway. Stops along his unknown journey, the cities in a new mental geography, just waiting to be invented. He looked at the girl a little more closely, and he had the sensation he might have seen her somewhere. He was careful not to ask her. He wouldn't have wanted to start his new life with any memories from the past, however unimportant. Still . . . He took courage and introduced himself, with a simple: "Nice to meet you. I'm Filippo."

"Alicia," the girl replied with a fleeting smile.

"That's not an Italian name . . ." The observation was idiotic in its banality, worthy of a small-town pickup artist. Maybe that's what he was, deep down.

"I'm Venezuelan," the girl explained, and Filippo was too shy to ask any other questions.

The train had begun to move. As soon as it pulled out of the station, it was swallowed up by the fog.

Filippo looked out the window. Maybe, who could say, the Northeast would become a land of farmers again, and Romania would become an industrial center infested by poison gases, with cities teeming with Italian immigrants.

"Do you mind if I pull down the shade?" he asked the girl sitting across from him.

"Be my guest. There's nothing to see out there anyway."

She had said it in that tough yet sweet tone that Latin Americans seem to have even when they talk about the weather. But maybe she really was angry, maybe she'd rebelled like he had, or maybe she was running away from something, or from someone.

Filippo pushed the button, and the curtain of coarse cloth was slowly lowered, a curtain coming down on that grim stage. On his past.

"Well, at least it's over," he thought, and it was the simplest thought he had ever formulated in his waking mind. He closed his eyes, eager to fall asleep, and without knowing why, he had the feeling that while his eyelids were lowered, the girl was watching him.

That was when, for the first time, Filippo smiled.

* * *

Antonio Visentin was stretched out on a leather sofa aboard the glittering yacht that served only as a way of justifying deductions for the Foundation's entertainment expenses. There was a bottle of cognac within reach. He hadn't stopped drinking since he'd boarded the yacht. After Francesco's phone call, he had gathered up the suitcases that he always had packed and ready; then he had driven to the port of Jesolo. He could hardly believe he had been caught. Right up until the end he had been confident that he could manage the situation without difficulties. Francesco would never suspect his father was the killer. But then something happened that he couldn't have foreseen. And now he had to escape. Not forever, of course. He would be able to arrange things, as he had always done in the past, but there was no way of fixing things with Francesco. His son was lost to him. He would have to learn to live with his hatred.

Through the silence he heard the noise of an arriving car.

He didn't move. He wouldn't have been able if he had tried. Too much cognac on an empty stomach.

The cabin seemed to be illuminated from within, from the gleaming reflections on the windows and the brass fittings. It was a little magic act that enchanted him for twenty seconds or so. When the headlights went dark, he heard two car doors slam in rapid succession. Sitting in profound darkness, he listened to the steps coming up the wooden gangplank.

The door swung open and the dazzling light blinded him. He threw up a hand to cover his eyes; through the outspread fingers he recognized Selvaggia, extremely elegant in her casual Hermès outfit. She looked as if she were ready to leave on a luxury cruise. The only detail that didn't fit in was the briefcase in her left hand.

"There's champagne chilling in the ice bucket," he told her. "To celebrate our departure."

Without taking her gaze off him, Selvaggia ordered her chauffeur to wait outside.

The alcohol made him analytical but kept him from trying to do anything. If he had moved, his head would have started spinning, and he would have wound up down on all fours, vomiting at Selvaggia's feet. And that could not be allowed to happen.

Selvaggia set her briefcase down on an armchair and walked over to him. She picked up the ice bucket; the ice had

melted into chunky water. She pulled out the empty champagne bottle and set it down. Then, in a single movement,
she grabbed the bucket and tossed the icy water into his face.
She did it with one hand, unemphatically, like a mother emptying her child's bucket into the sand before leaving the
beach.

The water on his face helped. He sat up, legs straddling
wide, his arms lying limp at his sides, his head dangling forward.

"So there weren't going to be any problems," she accused
him, slapping him flat-handed in the face.

Part of him reacted. He grabbed her wrist before she could
pull her hand away. He squeezed hard. Without anger, really
with the desperation of a man grabbing a ledge to keep from
falling.

"Let go of me," Selvaggia hissed.

He tried to focus on her.

"Let me go, I said!" The pain made her even more dicta-
torial.

He released her wrist.

Selvaggia jerked her hand away with an angry gesture.

"We have to set sail immediately. Everything's taken care of.
They're expecting us in Split, and from there they'll take us to
Romania."

Selvaggia sat down at his side, and changed her tone:

"It's about time for a Contessa to set foot in Romania again,
don't you think?"

That woman was incredible. She could make jokes at a
time like this. He wanted to kiss her, throw her down on the
sofa, ravish her, come all over her Hermès dress, prove to her
that he wasn't finished. He wanted to throttle her neck, he
wanted to wipe that smug grin off her face. He would have
liked to . . .

"I'm not coming," he managed to say. He had suddenly
changed his mind.

"Don't be an ass. Your little lawyer tricks aren't needed anymore. It's all over."

"I need to talk to Francesco," he replied stubbornly.

"To tell him what? That you're the swine who betrayed Alvise and that then you forced Giovanna to become your lover? And that then you killed her when she threatened to tell everything to him, to Francesco? Do you think that your son can understand you? Forgive you? No, Filippo hates me for much less."

The chauffeur poked his head in the door, speaking to Selvaggia like an aide-de-camp addressing his colonel on the eve of a major retreat.

"Contessa, we have to go."

Selvaggia nodded, understandingly.

"Start the engines."

The chauffeur nodded and discreetly closed the door behind him.

"I'm going ashore."

"Antonio," said Selvaggia in an attempt to instill some reason in his mind, "till now you've gotten away with it because what you've done is so inconceivable that your son has grabbed wildly at any possibility in order to avoid the truth. Now it's too late. If you can't accept that, then you might as well kill yourself."

He looked at her admiringly:

"I don't know where you get all this strength."

The chauffeur started the engines.

It was like an electric shock. Moving cautiously, he got to his feet and managed to take a few steps toward the door.

"Antonio!"

He turned around; she seemed miles away.

"What do you think you're doing?" she asked him, incredulous.

"I want to see my son," he said, his hand already gripping the brass doorknob.

The chilly salt air was like a second bucketful of water.

He must have been a pretty awful sight, considering the look that the chauffeur gave him as he resumed unmooring the boat.

His wobbly gait was not the result of the boat's pitch and roll. The swampy sea was motionless. He breathed deeply, gulping down fog and salt.

It was the air he had breathed since he was a child, an unhealthy air for anyone who hadn't been born in the Northeast. A swelling surge of water, perhaps the wake of a passing oil tanker in the distance, made the yacht pitch and yaw. He lost his balance and he felt the chauffeur grab his arm to steady him. He shook that unwanted hand away, and seized the railing of the gangway with all the determination that the boat's unbridled motion allowed him.

He set foot on solid ground with some satisfaction. For a moment, as he was crossing the gangway, he was afraid of pitching headfirst into the water. But he was Antonio Visentin, and the Visentins never fall.

He turned around to look at the yacht. The Romanian chauffeur was at the wheel, having pulled the gangway inboard. The boat was slowly heading out to the open sea.

Selvaggia didn't come on deck to bid him farewell. She was probably still sitting on the leather sofa. He thought he glimpsed the flickering flame of her Dupont lighter; she was probably lighting one of those cigars she loved so much. He had taught her to appreciate those Cuban cigars.

The engine revved and the yacht suddenly sped up; the bow rose in the water, and a yellowish wake spread out behind it. He stood gazing after the boat as it vanished into the nighttime mists. He wondered if he'd ever see Selvaggia again. One thing he knew for certain was that he'd never go see her in Timisoara. He wasn't going to abandon the Northeast, the way everyone else was about to do.

As the darkness tightened around him, he climbed into the Jaguar and phoned Francesco.

* * *

I had returned to town a while ago, and I was hunting for my father. Before turning him in to the police I wanted to talk to him. I had only one question for him: why? Why had he taken Giovanna to bed? Why did she consider him the man who had ruined her life? Why had he killed her? I was an emotional wreck, but the fury that filled my brain kept me from collapsing. That would happen later, when it was all over. I had gone to my father's villa, then to his law office, and even to the Villa Selvaggia. He wasn't anywhere. He must be hiding somewhere, or else he had fled with his accomplice. I was ready to follow him to Romania, but I was determined to make him answer my questions. I heard the muffled ring of the cell phone in my overcoat pocket. It was him.

"I have to talk to you," he said in a gummy voice.

"Don't think you can keep me from telling the police," I shouted. "You may be my father, but you're going to stand trial in a criminal court."

"I'll wait for you at the old iron bridge over the river."

It was an old bridge built by the Allies at the end of the war, to replace the one that the Germans had destroyed during their withdrawal. Papa and I used to fish from it. I wondered why he would choose that dark, cold, deserted place at that time of night.

In the distance, I saw the headlights of the Jaguar, the dome light burning brightly, the door wide open. I jabbed my foot down angrily on the accelerator and flicked on my brights.

Papa had one hand resting on the railing. His elegant tailored overcoat was unbuttoned, his tie was askew, outside the jacket. He was squinting against the bright beam of the headlights. He looked like a bewildered old man. The rage I had managed to tamp down until then became uncontrollable. I picked up rocks from the road and started hurling them at him. One hit him on the chest, another on the shoulder, a third on the forehead. He tried not to flinch as the rocks flew at him, then by instinct he raised one hand to protect his face.

I stopped about three steps away from him and picked up a particularly large rock.

"Why?!" I shouted. "Why?"

"She gave me no choice," he replied in a wavering voice. "She was going to tell you everything."

I lunged at him and knocked him to the ground. "Everything? What was she going to tell me?"

"She had figured out that Selvaggia and I had been responsible for Alvise's ruin," he replied, trying to get to his feet. "She started challenging me, in a subtle, twisted game. Before I knew it, we wound up in bed."

"Were you in love with her?"

"No. It was just a game. Giovanna loved only you."

"How could you?" I shouted.

I hoisted the rock high, ready to smash it down into his face. To kill him. Papa raised his hands to stop me.

"No! There's no need," he stammered, and then climbed up onto the parapet of the bridge.

"Don't be a coward," I shouted, trying to grab him.

He looked back for an instant, and then allowed himself to drop into the river. I heard a splash. Then silence.

I was trembling from the cold when I knocked at Carla's door. Carla let me in without a word. Teeth chattering, I told her everything that had happened, that my father had killed himself and that I was satisfied with that. Now I knew the truth, and no one else needed to know. The game was over.

Caressing my cheek, Carla said only: "Unless you tell the truth, you'll wind up like him."

That was when I burst into uncontrolled sobs, and with a voice that was nothing like my own, I burst out: "Now what about me? How will I ever be able to have a son? How can I . . . ever forget?"

Carla embraced me, with an infinite gentleness. I realized that she was weeping too, in silence.

"Come on," she said, "I'll come with you."

I went to the barracks and asked for Mele. The inspector took one look and realized that something very serious had happened.

"Call Zan," I said. "I have a statement to make."

The prosecutor took an hour to arrive. While we waited, I sat in silence, staring at the facing wall. Mele waited with me, standing beside me. Zan was annoyed at having been awakened in the middle of the night.

"I am all ears," he said, as he took a seat in the inspector's office chair.

"My father Antonio Visentin killed himself a little more than an hour ago. He jumped off the old iron bridge. Before committing suicide, he confessed that he had killed my fiancée, Giovanna Barovier, in a small suburban house and that he transported Giovanna's dead body to her own house in complicity with the Contessa Selvaggia Calchi Renier and her Romanian chauffeur."

Zan stared at me in horror.

"Please take down my official statement, if you would," I said.

"You're not in your right mind," Zan grumbled. "Maybe you should take some time to reflect . . ."

"Zan!" Inspector Mele exclaimed indignantly.

The prosecutor cleared his throat in embarrassment, then decided to take my testimony.

In reality, I didn't have much too add, but I wanted to make sure that every word was taken down with meticulous precision. I left the barracks a few hours later.

Carla was outside waiting for me. She flicked her cigarette away onto the wet asphalt and linked arms with me.

As we walked off into the dark, I felt a strange surge of strength. Strong enough to face the new situation. Strong enough to face the town.

* * *

"Glory be to the Father, and to the Son, and to the Holy Spirit. As it was in the beginning, is now, and ever shall be."

The rosary had just begun, and Don Piero's stentorian voice echoed through the half-empty church.

"World without end. Amen."

The prayer group that had assembled for Antonio Visentin's wake responded in a whisper that echoed like a gust of wind down the empty church aisles. No one, not even Francesco, wanted to pray for his damned soul.

Prunella was kneeling in the front row, dressed in black with a veil over her eyes. She had joined in the chorus mechanically, though the *incipit* of the rosary was especially well suited to her state of mind.

Glory be to the Father, and to the Sonj.

Alvise was dead. Giovanna was dead. Antonio was dead.

"In the first dolorous mystery we contemplate Jesus praying in the garden of Gethsemane," the elderly parish priest was reciting.

The first sorrowful mystery.

Mystery and sacrifice. This was the essence of violent and unjust deaths. Death is always unjust. The death of a daughter goes against nature. Prunella was alive, and she felt a profound sense of guilt. Her sin lay at the origin of that tragedy, of all that suffering. Years before, while her husband was in prison, she had gone to bed with Antonio Visentin, the family friend, the lawyer whose duty it had been to clear her husband's name. She had given her body to Visentin in order to take revenge for her husband's thousands of betrayals. And she had done it when Alvise most needed her, when he needed his wife, the woman whom he had led to the altar, who had embraced the sacrament of faithfulness and devotion. In sickness and in health, in good times and in bad. In poverty. That was why she could never forgive him. She had married the wealthiest man in town, and had abandoned him when he reduced her to poverty. Alvise had been her first and her last. Until Antonio, who had been her second and her last. With Alvise, it had lasted sixteen years. With Antonio, a few months. He had soon tired of her, of her overwhelming crises of guilt. Probably, he had taken her to bed with a finely calibrated goal, to alienate from Alvise the one person who might have fought on his behalf.

Alvise loved life, especially a life of luxury. He loved women, gambling, and reckless nights out with his friends. But he was no criminal. He would never have been capable of doing what they had charged him with, what they had convicted him of.

And yet she had chosen to believe the lies of scum like Giacomo Zuglio, the chilly logic of Antonio Visentin, and the hasty judgment of the town. She had chosen to believe the dispassionate but faulty decision of a judge. Her one shortcoming had been far more serious than Alvise's many shortcomings. Because, even though Alvise had betrayed her repeatedly, he would never have abandoned her. And that was precisely what she had done to him. She had repudiated him, and in so doing, she thought that she had rescued her own, skin-deep virtue.

"In the second sorrowful mystery we contemplate the scourging of our lord Jesus Christ in the house of Pontius

Pilate," Don Piero was reciting. His voice reached her from a distance, muffled by the buzzing of her thoughts.

Antonio had been her Pontius Pilate. He had done nothing to protect Alvise, his childhood friend, from the cruelties of flagellation. But what happened in the years that followed was even worse. And there was no justification imaginable. Even though she had turned her back on Alvise, the town had still turned its back on her.

And as she slipped into disgrace, she besmirched herself with her second sin. She had allowed herself to be devoured by envy. Envy of Antonio, and especially of Selvaggia. Selvaggia— that hateful, vulgar, arrogant, domineering, faithless woman who had commanded the town for years—the town's unquestioned queen. That untouchable woman, who could however touch anyone and anything that she pleased.

Prunella had become convinced that after Antonio left her, he had become Selvaggia's lover. And that had made her blind with fury.

"In the third sorrowful mystery, we contemplate the coronation of our lord with thorns."

When Giovanna, after all her grieving and suffering over her father, had finally started to rebuild her life, Prunella, instead of rejoicing in that process like any good mother, had fallen victim to a demented and all-enveloping jealousy. She couldn't stand the idea of Giovanna marrying either a Calchi Renier or a Visentin.

She had infused her daughter with the seed of suspicion. Over the course of the years, Prunella had managed to discover certain aspects of the truth. Don Piero had confided to her that Alvise was young Lucio's father. And a few years later, in the course of her work with the homeless and mentally ill, she had come to know El Mato, the town fool who wandered around dressed in an old parka shouting: "Now I understand! Now I've figured it out!" One summer day she went to visit

him in the lean-to where he lived in the country, to take him
some second-hand clothing. She had seen him washing himself
in a basin, and had seen the skin of his upper body, devastated
by old burns. Patiently, she had coaxed the story from him of
how he had gotten those burns. It was he who had set the fire
at the furniture factory. He had been paid by an emissary from
the Contessa, but he had never used the money. He still kept
the cash in an old briefcase hidden under his bed. Prunella had
watched as he rubbed those old fifty-thousand-lire banknotes
between his fingers. When he sloshed the gasoline over the
floor in the paint and varnish store room, he was falling-down
drunk, and the flames had enveloped him in a flash. The Contessa's emissary had taken him out of the country for medical
treatment. Then he'd come home, but he was never the same.
Prunella felt sure that the only reason they hadn't killed him
was that they no longer thought of him as a threat.

"In the fourth sorrowful mystery, we contemplate the climb
of Jesus up to Calvary's mount, bearing the exceedingly heavy
Cross."

She hadn't been honest with Giovanna. No, she certainly
hadn't. She'd been deceitful, insinuating and manipulative—as
only the envious know how to be. She had pushed her to dig
into the mystery, providing her with those few but fundamen-
tal truths, bit by bit. Giovanna's mental and emotional equilib-
rium was so fragile, the wounds of her abandonment had not
yet healed. But Prunella had plunged the knife of false hope
straight into her heart. And then, foolish woman that she was,
she had covered her eyes, turned her head away, pretended not
to know in what direction she had pushed her despairing
daughter. In the name of a truth that would never come out
into the open, she had driven her daughter into the darkness
of hell.

And now here she was, reciting the fifth sorrowful mystery,
in which we contemplate the crucifixion and death of Jesus on

the Cross. In order to plumb the depths of the mystery of a wretched wife and a deceitful mother. Of a woman who professed a sacred love in the pews of a church, so that she could conceal from herself her own inability to provide an unconditional love. Condemned to secrecy by her hypocrisy and pride. Cursed unto the ages of ages. Amen.

* * *

The reporter from *Romania Libera*, the most respected Romanian daily, waited for his photographer to finish his shoot of the Contessa Selvaggia Calchi Renier. He was in her office, in the new headquarters of the Torrefranchi Group in Timisoara. The reporter was overwhelmed by the elegance of the furnishings. The photographer began breaking down his lights, and the Contessa gestured to the reporter.

"I'm at your disposal," she said, with a smile.

The man smiled back and sat down across the desk from her.

"Why has an important group like Torrefranchi chosen to transfer its operations to Romania?" he asked.

"Because Romania is a country rich in natural and human resources, capable of offering numerous opportunities to a group as dynamic as ours."

"Here in Timisoara there are more than 1,200 Italian companies out of the 13,000 present in the country. One Italian newspaper called this a province of the Northeast. Do you agree with this statement?"

"It strikes me as inaccurate, inasmuch as we are only guests here," she replied diplomatically. "But the presence of northeastern Italian companies is unquestionably sizable. Most of the companies and most of the ten thousand Italians who live in Timisoara do come from that part of Italy."

"In an earlier interview you said that you were not satisfied with new Romanian labor regulations—"

"And I am still not satisfied. The regulations impose too many restrictions on the rights of companies to fire employees and negotiate salaries. If we hope to be competitive, we need to have an increasingly flexible labor market."

"Italy is Romania's largest trading partner, but it is only in sixth place in terms of investments—"

"The Torrefranchi Group has always adopted a different policy in this important sector. We have developed our industrial sites with special attention to the question of infrastructure, building new roads and repairing existing roads. And we take care of our own waste disposal. We are also making plans for a school and a nursery school for our employees."

"Free of charge?"

Selvaggia smiled. "Our prices are always very competitive."

"Many Italian industrialists complain about corruption among the authorities in Romania—"

"Corruption is a blight, harmful to Romania, and in particular to the customs sector. All we ask is reliable rules that will allow us to work without unreasonable risk."

"Now, a personal question: you have stated that you are the victim of a miscarriage of Italian justice—"

"A political conspiracy," the Contessa explained. "Like many of the investigations targeting entrepreneurs. But I am sure it will all be solved amicably. It's only a question of time."

About the Authors

Massimo Carlotto was born in Padua, Italy. He is the author of *The Goodbye Kiss* (nominated for the Edgar Award in 2007), *Death's Dark Abyss*, and *The Fugitive*, an autobiographical account of his time on the run after being falsely accused of murder. He is one of Italy's most popular authors and a major exponent of the Mediterranean noir novel.

Marco Videtta is a well-known screenwriter and the author of several successful Italian television series. *Poisonville* is his first novel.